THE SCENTED CHRYSALIS

The Scented Chrysalis

A novel
by

JOSÉ SOTOLONGO

BOOKS

Adelaide Books
New York / Lisbon
2019

THE SCENTED CHRYSALIS
A novel
By José Sotolongo

Published by Adelaide Books, New York / Lisbon
adelaidebooks.org

Editor-in-Chief
Stevan V. Nikolic

For any information, please address Adelaide Books
at info@adelaidebooks.org
or write to:
Adelaide Books
244 Fifth Ave. Suite D27
New York, NY, 10001

ISBN-10: 1-950437-71-X
ISBN-13: 978-1-950437-71-9

Printed in the United States of America

Contents

Mistrust all in whom the impulse to punish is powerful.

–Friedrich Nietzsche, *Thus Spoke Zarathustra*

The untold want, by life and land ne'er granted,

Now, Voyager, sail thou forth, to seek and find.

–Walt Whitman, *Leaves of Grass*

The fabled musk deer searches the world over for

the source of the scent which comes from itself.

–Ramakrishna

Chapter 1

The Underwear Hat

Once upon a time a young woman decided she wanted to have a child a month after she got married. She told her young husband about this decision in their small new house.

The young husband had some doubts about having a child, because he was unsure about their financial future. Although he wasn't timid, he was cautious, but he loved his wife very much, and he wanted to please her, so he agreed. This relieved the young wife, because she was determined to have a baby, and didn't want to stop contraception without telling him first, which she would have if necessary.

And so, one night soon afterwards the young woman and the husband coupled. An egg from the young woman's left ovary had been released that morning and travelled down the fallopian tube toward the uterus. One of the forty million spermatozoa that the husband had ejaculated swam from her cervix into the uterus, where the egg was making its way. By six the next morning the spermatozoa penetrated the egg's thin membrane. The spermatozoa released all its chromosomes into the egg, including one "Y" chromosome, which paired with the egg's "X" chromosome. The egg was now a male embryo!

The embryo divided into two cells by noon, and by dinner time the two cells had become four. Of course, the young woman had no idea what was happening, and wouldn't for several weeks. But in the meantime, the little embryo later that very day reached the uterus, which had been made plush by the young woman's hormones, and it attached itself.

It's important to know that any number of things could go wrong now. The lining of the uterus might be too thin, and the embryo would be flushed out of the woman without her noticing it the next time she got her period. Or the embryo might have died if one of the chromosomes wasn't perfect. But this embryo was lucky in every way, and it stayed put.

As expected, one of the chromosomes in the embryo, from either the spermatozoa or the egg (we can't be sure) carried instructions on how the brain would develop. The brain in the embryo grew normally, but the chromosome's instructions made a certain section grow differently than that of most other embryos. And so as the brain grew, the section that determined which gender the male embryo would be attracted to after birth grew bigger, and with different chemicals, than ninety percent of male embryos. Of course, the young woman wouldn't know this for many years to come.

After a few months, the embryo grew into a baby, and when it was born, the woman and the husband were amazed at its beauty and perfection. They could not believe their luck and had never been so happy.

Three years later, the young couple was still enraptured with their baby, which was now a beautiful blond boy.

One afternoon the boy was sitting on the floor of his mother's bedroom playing with his toys. He liked to watch his mother get ready for his father's arrival.

"What is that you're putting behind your ears?" he asked his mother, who was sitting in front of a mirrored dresser.

"Perfume." She looked at him in the mirror.

"Why?" he asked.

"To smell good," she replied.

"Why?"

"So your father will smell something nice when he gets home."

"Can I have some too?"

"No," she replied, "This one is for women. Men wear different perfumes."

"Why?"

"Because. Just like clothes are different for men and women, our perfumes are different."

Later, when his father came home, the young boy sat on his father's lap in front of the TV. The father liked the weight of his son's body on his lap. Every month it seemed a little heavier, and it was a comfort and a sadness to him that his son was growing and would some day be too big to sit on his lap.

The boy leaned back against his father's chest, and on his face he could feel his father's heat through the shirt and smell his father's deodorant. It made him want to get closer to him, and he put his arms around his father's chest, which brought his face near his father's armpit. The father became conscious of not raising his arm enough to let the smell of his sweat repel the boy.

"Is that your perfume?" the boy asked.

The father smiled at the TV, although the boy couldn't see it. "Yes. I guess."

The boy stretched his neck up to get his nose close to his father's ear.

"What are you doing?" his father asked.

"I don't smell it where mommy puts her perfume," the boy said.

His father laughed. "No. It's a deodorant. It goes under the arm."

"Why?"

The father hesitated, then said, "Because that's where body odor is strongest, and you want to cover it up."

"Why?"

"Because most people don't like it."

"I like it."

The father hugged the boy and changed the channel on the TV from the news to a children's show. He wanted to watch the news but he didn't want the boy to get bored and leave him. This was the best part of his day. He pulled the boy in closer and touched his nose to the corn silk hair, which smelled of honey and rain.

On the TV screen appeared a cartoon with blue dwarfs wearing floppy white caps. The little blue men were jumping up and down on a trampoline and the floppy caps would un-furl into long cones with each descent. The little boy laughed every time.

The next day the mother was loading the clothes washer near the kitchen and she dropped a few pieces on the floor. The boy picked one up. "What's this?" he asked.

"It's your father's underwear. It's just like yours, only it's white and bigger."

The boy held it up with two hands, and remembered the cartoon. He put the briefs on his head, but the waist was so much bigger than his head that it slipped down and covered his face. The smell struck him, surprised him with its newness, and he breathed it in.

"Silly boy," his mother said, laughing. She pulled the briefs off his head gently and put them in the washer.

"Why don't you put it on your head so you see what it smells like too?" the little boy asked.

"It's OK. I already know what it smells like."

He followed her into the bathroom, where she put the laundry bag back in the clothes hamper, and he saw that it was where the clothes were kept that smelled and would go into the washer.

Thereafter, the little boy would go to the clothes hamper to find his father's underwear and put it on his head. He would wear it while he played with his toys on the living room floor until his mother saw him and took it off him without reprimand. After a few days, his mother asked, "Why do you like to wear daddy's underwear on your head? Why not yours or mine?"

"Because I like how it looks."

And so when the little boy wore underwear on his head the mother and father laughed before they took it away. The little boy didn't cry when they did this, because he was making his parents laugh, and he knew he could go back to the hamper at any time.

But it happened that the mother had to go to the hospital for surgery, because early cancer cells were growing in her uterus, and it had to be removed. Because she was going to be in the hospital a long time, and the father had to go to work, the grandmother, who was the mother's mother, came to stay with them to take care of the little boy.

The grandmother was thin and had grey hair piled up on top of her head. Every time she spoke, her yellow teeth showed. When she arrived at the house and saw the little boy, she patted him on the head without smiling or kissing him and said, "Now, you won't be much trouble for your old grandma, will you lad?" The little boy didn't always understand what she said because she spoke differently than his mother and father.

"Why are your teeth yellow and all crooked?" the little boy asked the first night at the dinner table. She had made a pot of boiled beef and potatoes the little boy didn't like.

The grandmother stopped eating and looked at him.

"Son," the father said, "you shouldn't say things like that."

"But why aren't they white and straight like ours?" he persisted.

The grandmother got up and went into the kitchen. She came back to the table with a bar of soap. "You see this?" she asked the little boy. "We'll use it to wash out your mouth if you keep saying nasty things."

The father was not happy that the grandmother was threatening his son, but said nothing, because he needed her help taking care of the boy. Still, he gave the grandmother a disapproving look.

The little boy was not used to threats of harm or punishment, and he whimpered.

The father got up, even though he hadn't finished his dinner, and stood by the boy, putting a hand on his back. The boy cried louder. "It's OK son," the father said. "Nothing's going to happen to you."

The grandmother dropped her fork on the plate with a loud clang. "That child is too coddled. He needs to learn some manners."

"He's three years old." The father took the boy out of the dining room.

From then on the father and the boy had dinner in the living room, watching TV, while the grandmother ate in the dining room, reading a book.

"What is that on your head?" the grandmother asked the little boy the next afternoon before the father got home.

"It's my hat. I wear it every day."

When the grandmother realized it was the father's briefs, she rushed to the boy and snatched them off his head. She did this with such force that the little boy's head snapped sideways and he fell.

The grandmother ignored the boy's crying. "If I see you doing that again, I'll lock you in a dark closet. Do you understand?"

The little boy was still on the floor, crying, and didn't answer. The grandmother grabbed him by the arms and pulled him up to standing. She got her face close to his and said, "Did you hear me?"

The boy almost choked on her breath, because it smelled like garbage when it has been left too long in the kitchen. He nodded, still crying, and went to his room.

"That boy is a ninny," the grandmother said when the father came home and she told him what had happened. She did not think she was being too strict: she wanted her daughter's son, who was her own flesh and blood, after all, to grow up strong and normal and not bring shame to the family. She had never heard of a little boy wearing his father's underwear on his head, even for a minute, and could not abide it.

The father did not argue, and did not explain that he and the mother were aware of the boy's habit and didn't think it did any harm. He grew sad that he was forced to accept her behavior, and became even sadder when he remembered what the mother's doctors had said that morning: she would be in the hospital another two weeks.

The little boy was sad every day now, afraid of the grandmother. Even when his father came home he didn't play with
his toys in the living room while his father watched TV.

"Mommy will be home soon," his father told him. "Then
everything will be back to normal."

"When?" he asked.

"Soon," the father said. "Two weeks."

But this meant nothing to the little boy. He understood
today, and knew tomorrow came after you went to sleep, but
he didn't know what anything beyond that was. It might as
well be forever until he would see his mother again.

At last the two weeks passed, and the mother came home,
and the grandmother left.

After a day or so the mother noticed that the little boy was
not as happy and playful as he had been. She noticed that he
didn't put the underwear on his head any more.

"I just don't want to do it again," he said when his mother
asked him. "It reminds me of grandma and her yellow teeth."

But what the boy didn't say, because he was not even
aware of it, was that now every time he touched anything other
than his toys, he looked at his parents to see if they were going
to be angry with him.

That night, after the boy was asleep, the mother asked the
father what had happened with the underwear hat and the grandmother, and the father told her and wept, because he thought he
had been weak in not defending his son against the old woman.
The mother put her arms around him and said that he had done
the best he could, given the situation. As they hugged in silence,
they each resolved different things: the father that he would mold
his son into someone who would not be at risk for ostracism, and
the mother that she would not thwart her son in any way, so long
as he did no harm. Their boy would live happily ever after.

Chapter 2

A Child's Football

He fell in love with football at the age of seven, in 1990.

"Come sit with me, buddy," his father said to Lucas in the living room watching a football game on TV.

He liked it when his father, usually too busy with his law practice, took time to be with him. Lucas looked forward to weekends, the only time his father was not buried in work.

"What are they doing?" Lucas asked as he watched the screen. He was standing by his sitting father, leaning on his knees. When his father spoke, the boy could feel the vibration of the voice through the man's legs and into his own ribcage. He leaned in harder.

"Playing football."

"Why is that man putting his hand in the rear of the man who's bending over?"

"That's how they put the ball in play. The man in front bending over is the center, and he passes the ball between his legs to the man behind him, and he's the quarterback."

"Why can't they just face each other?"

"It's just how the game is, Luke. Let's watch."

Lucas watched a few minutes. "Why can't the man in back put his hands lower, not so close to the other man's rear end?" he asked when the ball was being snapped again. The men in blue and grey uniforms were doing this over and over again.

"It's just how they do it, Luke."

"Mom said not to let anyone touch me like that. So how come those men are doing that?"

"It's different in football, Luke. It's okay when they're playing football."

He couldn't take his eyes off the screen. He sat on the rug in front of the recliner and used his father's shins as a backrest.

"I want to play football," he said to the TV after a few minutes.

Jerry chuckled. "Okay. We'll get you a ball, and I'll teach you." He leaned forward, rubbed Lucas' head, and left his hand there.

"Will mom be okay with it?"

"Of course. Why shouldn't she?"

He stayed silent. He wanted to play this game, learn it from his father, even if his mom might not like it.

During his first lesson with his father in Central Park, two blocks away, he learned to catch and throw, and did it well. He wanted to play this game in which men, in colorful uniforms like a marching band, but wearing helmets like aliens from space, pushed and grabbed each other, and touched one another in ways that men usually did not. And while he learned this game, he would have the attention from his father that he craved, without distractions.

"Dad's teaching me football," he said to his mother the next day. He watched her face for disapproval.

"I know. He told me yesterday." She was in the kitchen putting groceries away. "He said you went to the park and were throwing the ball back and forth, and running passes, and everything."

"It's okay with you that I play?"

"Of course. It's a great sport. Just don't get hurt."

He joined a junior football team that played weekends in Central Park, and both his parents went to see him play. He loved putting on his red helmet and uniform, white with red lettering. And he liked that he didn't have to throw himself at the other players like the men on TV, just touch them, and that it was okay to do so just about anywhere on their bodies. He could hear Jerry's voice cheering every time he touched a boy from the other team carrying the ball. Lucas put his hands on the boys near the buttocks, not on the upper back, like the other boys did.

He played regularly through elementary and middle school, and years later, in high school, when the game changed to tackle, he enjoyed playing even more. As he matured into his father's tall, wide frame, most of the other players were no match for his strength, mass, and tenacity. When he tackled an opposing team player, and both fell to the ground, faces inches away, he would take in the other teen's breath and smells, and would hold on to him tight and long, until he heard the referee's whistle.

Lucas particularly enjoyed tackling Alex, a tight end from the neighboring school. He had sandy hair and a chipped front tooth, and his muscular waist twisted like a python under the grip of Lucas's forearms. Alex's body smelled of raw chicken and butter, and his face never turned towards Lucas, who still managed to breathe in Alex's exhaled air.

He knew the other boys did not lock their arms around each other, that he was never tackled and held as long as he did the others, an urge he could feel between his legs. He had heard from his team-mates the derogatory remarks about faggots and homos, and did not believe he was one of those. He didn't see a connection. The embarrassing Gay Pride marches and the AIDS epidemic that had killed so many gay men were all over the news on TV, and this is not who he was. But, aware that he felt something for his teammates that the other boys probably did not, he had looked up "homosexuality" in the school's library, and had read about normal young men experimenting sexually with each other. He was comfortable doing this embracing and having what he thought of as normal urges, so long as he was seen as a regular guy and the other boys did not object.

Coach Gomez called him into his office after one of the first games of the season in his sophomore year. Carlos Gomez, with his bushy black mustache and Notre Dame cap, sat behind his bare metal desk, and spoke in a smooth voice, not with the gravelly shout he used on the field. He kept his eyes down on his desk.

"There's been some complaints about your tackling, Luke."

Lucas frowned, not understanding what anybody could be complaining about.

"The coaches from the other teams have told me, three times now, that when you tackle their guys you hold on to them too long, and that your face gets too close to theirs." Coach Gomez paused and cleared his throat, eyes still fixed down on his desk. "It's making some of those guys uncomfortable."

Lucas felt a prickling sensation on his upper lip, and sweat starting to build in his armpits. "I just tackle them and hold them until I hear the whistle." His voice was close to a whisper, barely reaching the coach across the desk.

Coach Gomez kept looking down at the desk, which had no papers on it. "I'm having a meeting with the other coaches tomorrow. They're saying I have a pervert on my team, and I have to set them straight. But from now on, just ease up, will you?" Then he stood up, walked Lucas to the door of his office, and closed it behind him.

"Is there something wrong at school, Luke?" his father asked a few days later. He was in jeans and held some legal folders, on his way to the living room, where he did work in the evenings. Rose was in the kitchen making dinner, but the pass-through into the dining area, where Lucas was doing homework, was open.

"No, Dad. Everything's okay. Why?"

"Your mother got a call at the gallery from school this afternoon, saying that Coach Gomez wants to meet with us."

Lucas had a feeling of dread, remembering the conversation with the coach.

"I don't know what it could be." He avoided his father's eyes.

A few days later, on Saturday, Rose told Lucas that they wanted to talk to him when Jerry got back from tennis.

"What's it about?"

Rose hesitated. "We met with Coach Gomez yesterday. We'll talk later."

Later in the living room, Rose sat in an armchair in her usual blue jeans and sweatshirt. Jerry sat with Lucas on the sofa and re-counted Coach Gomez's concerns. His father spoke haltingly, as if unsure he wanted to talk at all.

Lucas kept his gaze on the heavy green drapes of the windows and didn't look at his father much, but when he did he saw discomfort. His father's eyebrows were scrunched down in a frown, his mouth pursed downward. When Lucas glanced at his mother, who had remained quiet, he saw that she hadn't moved, and her face was calm. She appeared querying, head tilted to one side, eyes soft on Lucas.

"Why have you been playing like that, son?" Jerry mumbled, looking down at his slippers.

"It's just how I play, dad." His voice was a hoarse whisper. He knew he could not describe the thrill he felt when he got close to the other men.

"He said he spoke to you about this already?"

"Yes, Dad, he did. And I told him I wasn't going to play that way anymore."

Jerry glanced at Lucas's face before looking away again. "Well, that's good. But unfortunately, he wants to suspend you from the next three games."

"No!" Lucas wailed, his eyes wide. This couldn't be. "But Dad," he gasped, "I told him I wasn't going to play like that any more!"

"I know son, but he said that the other coaches won't play his team if this happens again. He's worried about his reputation, said he has to punish you to show the other coaches he means business."

Lucas looked down but could see nothing. His eyes were clouded over, and for a few seconds he could hear nothing, as if in a black, sound-proof bubble.

"I'm sorry, Luke," Jerry said, going towards the adjoining den, where he did paperwork. "We tried to change his mind, but he said he had to do this." He closed the door behind him.

At that moment, the world revealed itself in a new way, and he felt a grey veil of shame for what he desired settling over him. How could something he felt so deeply and so unequivocally merit punishment? When he looked up, he saw that Rose had remained poised, hadn't moved her legs or her hands, still on her lap. Trying not to cry, he got up to go to his room, and his mother said, "Lucas, come here" in a low voice. She held out her hand, palm up, and he reached out for it. He clasped it and stood leaning into her. Her arms went around his waist and held him tight. He read this as pity, or perhaps sympathy, neither one of which he wanted from her. What he wanted was her approval and admiration as if he were an adult, not to be comforted, as if he were a child. He felt diminished, and yet this support felt good, certainly better than his father and the coach's disapproval. He wished he hadn't given in to his desires, didn't have the need to do something that deserved punishment.

When Rose let go of him, she looked up at his face, and he saw in her eyes sadness, although she was trying to smile. He went into the kitchen for a glass of water, an overwhelming cloud of humiliation surrounding him. His vision was still clouded, but he noticed a paring knife on the counter, left over from the dinner prep. He picked it up to put it in the knife block, but instead studied its sharp edge, and brought that potential source of death to his wrist. Wasn't that what men who wanted to die honorably after being disgraced had done since Roman times? He pressed his thumb on the edge to test its sharpness harder than he meant to, and saw his blood dripping from the blade on to the counter. He rinsed the knife in the sink, took some paper towels, and stanched the bleeding before going to his room. He didn't want to alarm his mother and create a scene. She was still sitting in the same chair without a book or the TV on, looking at the heavy green drapes behind which he had played hide and seek with her as a child. He made sure to put his hand with the bloody paper towel in his pocket as he walked past her.

In his room, he wept, and got some consolation from re-solving that he would never again engage in shameful socially unacceptable behavior. He had no doubt that years from now he would look back on today as a turning point.

Chapter 3

Vassar

Lucas's mother Rose suggested they visit Vassar College, although he had been considering only colleges in New York City. "It can't hurt just to look at it, Luke," she said. "You've never lived anywhere but New York." College was still more than a year away.

"Take an extra dress shirt," Rose said as she bustled around, helping him pack for the trip to Poughkeepsie, two hours north of their large apartment in Manhattan. "We may be able to get into the Culinary Institute for dinner. It's close to Vassar, and from what I hear, business hasn't recovered after 9/11." He took a plaid dress shirt hanging in his jumbled closet and began to fold it when Rose said, "Let me do it. I don't want you to look like you're wearing origami."

Lucas smiled and wrapped his arms around her from behind. His height and his burly shoulders, muscled from years of football and weight-lifting, all but made Rose's five-foot figure vanish. He took in the fragrant lavender water she used after a shower.

On the ride to Poughkeepsie the next day, he insisted on driving. It was just the two of them. "I'll get us there faster, mom," he said, holding his palm up for the keys. They walked into the garage under their building.

Rose commandeered the radio as soon as he had turned the engine on. "No rock music while you drive, Mr. Speedy," she said, and tuned in a classical station.

"Why don't you like the idea of my going to college in New York?" He asked as he steered the car on to the West Side Highway.

She turned the radio down, and took a few seconds to answer. "There's another world beyond New York, you know. There's no telling what's going to happen here next."

"What do you mean?"

"Your father thinks the attack on the World Trade Center is only the beginning." She looked out the window at the skyline. "And I think he may be right. He and I are tied to New York, because he's got his law practice and I've got my gallery, but you don't have to be here necessarily."

"Nothing's going to happen here, Mom. That was a fluke, that attack. It's been nine months."

"Eight. I hope you're right. But no point your taking unnecessary risks." She turned the radio off. "You know, mothers want to protect their offspring. Preservation of the species. Besides, I think it'd be good if you spent some time outside of New York." She paused and then added, "It'd be nice if you met someone special, and maybe being out of the city, away from us a little, will make it easier for you." She glanced at him.

"I have nice friends in New York." He steered the car into the ramp towards the Taconic Parkway.

"I know," she said, "but that's not what I mean. I haven't seen you date anyone in high school yet. Maybe New Yorkers aren't your type, or you need to be more on your own to date someone."

"I know a lot of nice people in school," he said. "We all just like to go out in groups, that's all."

"But people in high school still date-one-on one, right?"

"Some do."

"Not you, though."

"Mom, lay off, please. Not everyone is the same," he said in a quiet voice.

"Yes, I know." Rose kept her eyes straight ahead. "What's the name of that song that goes, 'Different strokes for different folks?'" When Lucas said nothing, she added after a brief glance, "I can see your eyes rolling from here."

Lucas laughed out loud, but said nothing.

"The only thing about Vassar is," Rose said after a minute, "I don't know if they have a decent football team."

"I already looked them up. They don't have a football team at all."

"At all? So that's a problem for you, then."

"No, not really," he said, clenching the steering wheel. "I'm giving it up after high school anyway."

Rose frowned. "How come?"

"Oh, it's time," he said.

Her frown deepened, and she turned to look at him without having to twist her neck. "It wouldn't have anything to do with that incident with Coach Gomez, would it?"

Lucas's lips tightened, but he didn't want to display his annoyance at the reminder of that humiliating, hurtful episode. He opened his mouth to relax it. "No, Mom. I've just had enough of it. Why don't you turn the radio back on? The music was relaxing." He flashed his brights at a slow driver ahead, even though it was daytime.

Out of the corner of his eye, he saw his mother shaking her head. Was she disappointed that he was giving up football? His mind flashed back to the afternoon a year ago when they had sat in the living room and talked about Coach Gomez, and his mood, which had started upbeat at the prospect of a road trip with Rose, darkened for the rest of the trip.

They didn't talk much the rest of the ride up to Pough-keepsie, except for Rose reading to him from some brochures about the history and architecture of the college. When they arrived and drove in through the gates, he was struck by the splendid looks of the campus, and his mood brightened again. He looked at Rose and smiled that day in May of 2002.

After they finished their meetings with admission officers and faculty at Vassar, Lucas and Rose strolled under the dogwoods and magnolias, which were starting their spring display. Rose marveled at the elaborate architecture of the library. "I envy you." She put her arm around his as they stood in front of it, admiring the portico. "I wish I could go to school here, surrounded by all this beauty."

"I'm looking forward to it," Lucas said. And then he murmured, "I'm going to miss playing in a team sport, though." He was going to miss was not just the game of football, but the physical closeness to the other men, even when it wasn't sexually arousing.

"I thought you wanted to give all that up." She looked into his face.

"No. Mainly just football."

"The men's volleyball team is supposed to be very good here," Rose said after a moment.

Lucas made a face. "That's not a real man's sport."

She chuckled. "Why don't we look into a school with other varsity teams, then?"

"No, it's okay. I'm done with organized sports. It's over." He started walking back to the car. Rose stayed where she was and watched his broad back, shaking her heard again.

He had come to the decision to give up football over the course of many months, after the conversation with Coach Gomez and then his parents that afternoon, over a year ago. He would continue playing through high school, he had decided — he would give himself that; but he would not go to a college where football or any other contact sport was even a possibility. He didn't want the temptation as he entered adulthood. That desire for sexual experimentation he had read about hadn't left him yet, but it was time to leave certain things from his youth behind.

After they were done driving around the Vassar campus, they went to the small hotel to check in and change for dinner. At the front desk, staffed by a young man in a jacket and tie, Rose insisted on separate rooms; Lucas didn't see the need. "We can share a room for one night, mom."

"Nonsense. We should have our privacy. And who knows, you might get lucky." She smirked and glanced at the young man behind the desk.

Lucas blushed, and he saw that the cheeks of the young man across the desk also colored. He noticed then that the man was wearing a shirt underneath his black blazer that was identical to one he owned: ochre with thin blue stripes. The shirt matched the man's hair color, as it did Lucas', and he could detect from across the desk that the man was wearing Halston cologne, inexpensive, but one of his favorites.

"Thank you, Cole," Rose said as they finished the check-in. It was then that Lucas noticed the man's name on the lapel pin.

"Nice young man," Rose said in the elevator on the way to their rooms. Lucas had thought so too, but he shrugged and said nothing.

They were able to get a table for dinner a couple of hours later at the Culinary Institute, which normally required reservations weeks in advance. Rose had been right about the impact of the collapse of the twin towers eight months before, even this far from New York.

Their server at dinner that evening was one of the students, a heavy-set young woman dressed in a black uniform, appropriate for the elegant dining room, with brocade curtains and chandeliers. She had a round, rosy face underneath short brown hair. "This is my last rotation," she said when Rose asked her how long she had before graduation, "so I'll be finished in six weeks." She looked mostly at Lucas, whose shoulders towered over the back of the Chippendale chair. "We all rotate through waiter service at some point," she said.

"Do you have a job yet?" asked Rose.

"Oh, yes. I have two offers right in this area. New York City is still sort of dead right now."

"Yes, I know. And what's your name?" Rose asked.

"Heather." The young woman moved around the table adding spoons for the soup course.

"Well, Heather, Lucas will hopefully start at Vassar next year." Rose placed her hand on his forearm. "So we might run into you again in one of the local restaurants."

"Vassar is a great school — beautiful," the woman said as she looked at Lucas and refilled his water glass. Lucas noticed that the pants of the black uniform she wore were too tight across the wide hips, and he thought he got a hint of body odor when she got closer to him than she needed to pour the water. He pretended to stifle a yawn.

After dinner Lucas drove them back to the hotel, and found he was not at all tired. The coffee after a late meal was still having its effect, although it was near eleven.

"I think I'll go to the bar and have a soda, Mom. I'm not sleepy yet," he said to Rose as they entered the small hotel. There were no guests in the small lobby, the gurgling of a tiny fountain in the center the only sound. There was now a young woman behind the reception desk.

"Sure, honey. But don't be too late. We're driving back early tomorrow morning." She kissed his cheek goodnight.

He entered the dimly lit bar, heavy with dark wood paneling. The counter was deserted except for a man sitting on a stool. The bartender stood and watched the baseball game on TV.

He took a seat at the bar a few feet from the other customer and ordered a soda. Out of the corner of his eye he saw that the man sitting at the bar looked at him and walked towards him. In the dim light he saw it was Cole, from the front desk earlier that day.

"Mind if I join you?" He didn't wait for an answer before sitting down.

"No, it's fine," Lucas said. "You're off work?" He noticed that Cole's jacket and tie were off, the sleeves of his striped rolled up, and he was having a beer. Close up he could see that Cole was several years older than him, perhaps mid-twenties. The Halston scent was still there, but mellower, sweeter, and Lucas wondered where Cole wore it that the fragrance would still be radiating with his body heat this late in the day.

"Yeah. I like to wind down before I go home," Cole said. "How was your visit to Vassar?"

"Fine." Lucas looked at him. "But how do you know that's where we went?"

Cole smiled. "After you checked in and went upstairs this afternoon, your mom came back to the lobby to talk to me." He paused and glanced at Lucas. "She wanted to know what social life was like for young people in this area."

Lucas smiled, shook his head. "Yikes. Good old Mom. So what did you say?"

"I told her I don't really know because I'm not in this area full time." He sipped his beer. "I work in New York, and I come here twice a week to take a couple of classes at Vassar. So I work a few hours here at the hotel every week to make extra cash." He paused. "She seems very nice, your Mom. Worried about her son," he smiled, looking at his beer, then at Lucas.

"Yeah, I guess. So what kind of work do you do in New York?" Lucas signaled the bartender for another soda.

"Oh, I'm self-employed. It's a lot more money than I could make if I just stayed around here and worked full time."

"What do you do in New York that earns so much money?" Lucas asked.

Cole looked away, asked the bartender for another beer when the man brought Lucas's drink, then said, "Oh, I'm not sure you want to know."

"What do you do, rob banks?" Lucas snickered.

Cole smirked. "Well, no. But it's not conventional work, either, I can tell you that."

Lucas waited, keeping his eyes on Cole. "So? What is it?"

Cole smiled and looked around briefly, to confirm that there was no one within earshot. "I hustle."

It took Lucas a few seconds to get it. "You mean, like sex?" he whispered, even though the bartender was watching TV at the far end of the bar.

Cole nodded. "It's great money. I don't even need this job in the hotel, really," he said. "I'm like just trying to save as much as possible before I go back to Vassar full time."

The bartender brought the soda, and Lucas sipped it and looked at Cole in the mirror behind the bottles of liquor. "So women pay you to have sex with them?" He had heard of this, but this guy was not how he imagined a hustler would look like or behave.

Cole shook his head. "Not quite." He paused. "I do men."

Lucas sat up straight on his barstool. "Huh?" Lucas looked around to see if anybody was listening. "So you're gay?" he said through a grimace, and Cole nodded.

Lucas brought his drink closer to him, almost hugging it to his chest, and wiped his dry mouth with a paper napkin. "I never would have known from looking at you, when you were at the registration desk. Not just the hustling part. I mean the gay part."

"Well," Cole said, "we're just regular people, those of us who do this. Like sex work, I mean. The money's good, and it's a job. Although I could tell you some stories," he chuckled and shook his head.

"What do you mean?" Lucas turned now in his bar stool to face Cole. "Like weirdoes? Dangerous stuff?"

"Not much dangerous stuff, no." Cole spun his beer around slowly on its coaster. "Just like… interesting encounters I've had. Some very strange ones, actually."

"Like what?' Lucas was ignoring his soda now.

Cole looked at him square on. "You sure you want to hear this?"

Lucas just nodded, frowning, eyes fixed on Cole. He had never met anyone like this. This was just a regular guy, a slightly older version of himself, exactly how he might imagine himself in a few years. He pulled his barstool closer to Cole.

Chapter 4

Cole

There were four calls that afternoon, all asking for appointments for that very day. I had to juggle the schedule around to accommodate them all.

I don't usually have a problem getting hard two or three hours after my last come, but less time than that and I risk failure, which means disappointment for the client, which means not only no tip, but no repeat business. And two thirds of my clients are regulars. About half of the regulars are married to women.

I also like to shower between clients, which means getting home to Chelsea, which can take some time. I shower because for the client, it's like I'm only his for the day, maybe even virginal-like, and when we're done, since there's many times that things can get wild, I get pretty messy.

Eventually I won't be doing this any more. I'm not just covering living expenses now, I'm putting some cash away to finish college. I did two years and couldn't swing it financially any more, so here I am. When I go back to school, computer programming is what I'll take up. I don't have a passion for it but that's where the world is going, right? Anyway, this sex work is so mechanical anyway, also without passion. Totally meaningless, which is fine and it's the only way I want it.

So this guy calls like at two in the afternoon — he's a first-timer, and he sounds young, and like really shy and scared. When I ask him how old he is he says twenty-four, which is a little older than me, and I'm wondering why this young guy is needing my services. I figure he's maybe married to a woman and he's trying to sort himself out. We agree we're going to meet at ten that night, and he wants me to go to his place, so I say OK. I don't pack heat, and I've never gotten in trouble in three years of doing this, but if a place looks dicey I don't even ring the doorbell. I also stick to good neighborhoods in Manhattan only — no outer boroughs, no tenement buildings. Most of the time, though, I meet the guys in hotels that know me and appreciate the business.

My second job of the day is at seven, with a regular at a hotel. It's great that this middle-aged gay guy is a quickie always, and because he knows the game we don't have to waste a lot of time with explanations or other bullshit, like how do you like it, do you want me to do this or that, all that stuff. This guy is also not bad looking, although he's like twice my age. Believe me, that helps. I hate having to close my eyes when I'm working the goods.

So I'm out of there by eight plus, get home and shower, catch up by phone with my sister in Albany and head out to the young guy's place in the east seventies, a boring but safe, posh neighborhood. I dress in a long sleeve pink Façonnable shirt and black jeans.

When I get to the building the doorman looks at me like, what the fuck do you want, but he calls the guy on the handset and lets me pass, and even tells me where the elevator is and what floor the guy is on.

So when this client opens the door, I'm like stunned. This guy is beautiful. He has softly curly brown hair around like a perfect face, with a narrow, straight nose, high cheekbones and big brown headlights with lashes out to here. And he has the sweetest, kissing lips I've seen in a long time. Some of these guys with pretty faces are pudgy down below, but this guy is not only not fat, he looks trim and in shape and he's a little taller than me.

I follow him into this really nice living room, with green satin upholstery on the furniture that matches the drapes, and all the lights are on. There's a lot of artwork on the walls, not prints or posters, either, and he asks me to sit down and do I want anything to drink. I say no to the drink but I sit on the sofa so maybe he'll sit next to me and we can begin the prelims at least, because I've got a one o'clock in the Village, and this guy is so mellow and I'm so like punched by his looks that I may actually get a kick out of this one and it means I definitely will have to shower afterwards.

But he sits in a big armchair across from me and starts asking me what the first timers always ask: is Cole my real name, where am I from, how long have I been doing this. So after I dance around the truth for a while I say, would you like to get started, and his eyes open wide and he gets a little pale and swallows hard, and when he speaks I can barely hear him.

That's when he tells me that he's never had sex before, and that in fact no one except his doctors have ever seen him naked, because he was born with a problem that needed lots of surgery, and nothing looks normal below his waist. I look at his legs and they seem OK, and I automatically look at his crotch without meaning to, as if I could see through his pants, dumb fuck that I am, and this guy turns red, and he says you know, maybe I'll just pay you and we're done, I don't want to go through with this.

But I'm thinking, this is a nice guy, in a nice apartment, and he's easy on the eyes. Shit, it'd be nice to have him as a regular, so I say, why don't you pay me now, OK, but let's not waste it, why don't we go into the bedroom and just take it slow, and we don't have to do anything you don't want.

So now he looks relieved, a little, and he takes cash from his pocket and hands it to me, and I make sure that my fingers caress and linger on his for not even a second, but it's enough, that touch, and I see his shoulders relax and he takes me to the bedroom by the hand, which is sweet, but no savvy client ever does it. The bedroom is all blonde wood, and the halogen lights are dimmed, but I can see that nothing is out of place.

I take off my shoes and I ask him if he wants me to undress, and he swallows hard again and just nods; he looks like he can't speak. His eyes are like big shiny buttons. I strip down to my underwear and start rubbing my crotch to get things going, looking at his face, and I ask him doesn't he want to take something off. So he nods again and takes off his shirt, and his chest looks good, not super built up, but lean and tight, and it's good enough that I get an easy, extra hardness with the help of my hand.

I walk up to him and bring my face close to his, and even though I don't go in for kissing on the job, because I only get anything out of a kiss when it's someone I'm really into, like my present boyfriend Raul, I think, what the hay, if he wants to, it's OK, because he's so hot.

I start to unbuckle his belt and he gently takes my hands away, so I step back a couple of feet and drop my briefs, and he gasps at what I've got. So I ask him, don't you want to try to go a little further. Because in my head I know I want to come back, but I don't want to push him.

He doesn't say anything, this guy, he just looks like he's going to cry, but he forces himself to undo his pants and drop them, and you can just see the pain in his face, but he looks down at the floor, won't look at me when he's down to his briefs.

His skin below the belly-button is like one big up and down scar that looks like a long crater, with fleshy red welts streaking out to the surrounding skin, like thick scars from old stitches, and the hollow in the center is so deep it looks almost like a big open vagina, and now I'm thinking so what, I can deal with this, I've seen scars before, though not so huge. So I move up to him slowly and hook my thumbs on the elastic of his underwear but don't pull them down right away, in case he really doesn't want me to, but he doesn't fight it, and I pull them down to his thighs and then look down to see what's what so I can get to work.

The deep crevice below the waist continues on down into this guy's small dick, which is almost completely split in two and looks like an index finger fileted open down the middle. There is regular skin on the sides of this thing but that center groove is all pink, like the inside of your piss hole, like this has to be super sensitive, and underneath, his balls are two little sacs that you couldn't even cup with your hand.

I always try to be professional no matter what a client looks like down there, and although I try this time, he sees the look on my face, and on his I see mostly hurt and shame, but also anger, and I know it's over. But I step back, trying to recover, and I say, do you want us to lie down, in as soft a voice as possible, and he closes his eyes and shakes his head no, and now his lids are tight closed but leaking.

I almost get dressed and get going, because it's getting late now and I've got the one o'clock, but I don't like to leave a client unhappy, and this guy is hurting. By now I've way lost my hard-on, but I can see sex is not what this was about, so I take him by the hand and lead him to the bed, put my hands on his shoulders and gently push him down on it, and lift his legs off the floor on to it. Then I lie down next to him and just hold him for a while. And before I leave ten minutes later I do something I've never done before, which is I kiss him on both cheeks, and then I lick the wetness that is seeping down his lashes and from the canyoned finger down below.

But I never see him again. It's a good thing he doesn't call, because I need the money, but I love Raul, and like I said, I like to keep things clean.

Chapter 5

The Law and Oscar Wilde

Lucas, throughout Cole's anecdote, had been shocked into silence at the details of what he heard. The matter-of-fact narration of what seemed to Lucas an astonishing encounter had mesmerized and intrigued him.

When Cole finished speaking, he swigged the last of his beer. "Well, gotta go. Early class tomorrow."

Lucas, despite the queasy feeling that had built up while Cole spoke, wanted him to stay. He wanted more. He wasn't sure whether he wanted to hear the story again, or know more about Raul, Cole's boyfriend, or explore Cole's feelings about the encounter he had just narrated. Maybe it was all of those. All he knew was that this man, upstanding and masculine, was not like any other he had met. His almost hypnotic state prevented him from speaking until Cole stood up.

"You have to go?"

Cole smiled. "Yeah. I'd better."

Lucas saw in that smile and in those eyes an interest, a connection. "I guess, if you have school tomorrow." He didn't know what else to say, how to make this man stay. He had to stop himself from grabbing Cole's arm to stop him as he waved to the bartender and paid his bill.

Cole extended his hand, but Lucas hesitated. The handshake was good-bye, but he took the man's hand and felt his firm, almost painful grip. He watched as Cole left the bar, and afterwards felt so alone he wanted to weep.

Back in his room, he stood in the bathroom and looked at himself in the mirror. The fluorescent lights overhead made his face look older. Where would he be when he was Cole's age? Would he, by then, have left these desires behind, outgrow them and watch them recede? Would he have the confidence to act on them before he became a full adult and had to find a woman to live with and marry? He felt an urgency to explore that part of himself that had only brushed him while playing football. But what if that really was what he was, a gay man like Cole, who looked and acted straight? No, he was not in that category, despite his fascination with Cole's story. Being gay was not something his father or his friends in the football team would ever approve of. And yet — wasn't his mother sending hints that she wanted him to find himself, be whatever he was supposed to be? Did she really know what he was feeling, or was he just projecting attributes to her that he found reassuring?

He went to bed, frustrated by the lack of answers, and tried to think about which sports he would pursue now, and about dinner at the Culinary Institute, but his mind wandered back to the conversation at the bar. He had always assumed that men who had sex with other men would be easy to spot, have a way of speaking or dressing that would give them away and invite ostracism. Primping pansies, he had read once in an old book about sexual disorders he had found in the library, referring to homosexual men. But this Cole was just a regular guy studying to be a computer programmer, not a fashion designer or a hairdresser. After an hour, as he fell asleep, he made a mental note to buy himself some Halston cologne when he got back to New York.

The next day, on the drive back home, Rose asked about his evening after she went to bed.

"Oh, fine. I had a couple of sodas in the bar. Ran into Cole, the guy from the reception desk."

"Really?" She sounded happy, and had a wide grin. "So? What did you do?"

"We just talked."

"You stayed in the bar?"

"Yeah. No place else to go, really."

Rose paused. "Well. You could have gone out to another place, more lively. Or gone back to your room, or his place."

"Why? We just wanted to talk. The bar was fine."

"He was very good looking," she said. Rose said nothing for a few minutes, then she turned the radio off. "I don't want to meddle, Luke. But I really hope you start having some dates, some romantic interests. It's what young men your age do. Just be careful about having safe sex."

"Mom." Lucas clenched his jaw. "I'm not ready for that."

"Okay. Like I said, I don't want to poke my nose in your business. I just want you to be happy. Go out and have fun with whomever you want. Don't make yourself fit a mold that isn't you."

For the rest of the ride home, he mulled her comments over. He was grateful to her for her encouragement, but, if he understood what she was saying, she was making assumptions about what he wanted that were not correct.

That summer he met buddies from the football team in the park and threw the ball around, played some scruffy games.

He tried not to think about Cole, but the man's image kept appearing unexpectedly — while watching TV, listening to music, reading. Cole's words and personality resurfaced again and again and made him want to turn the clock back so that he could prolong their meeting, maybe do as Rose had mentioned, go to Cole's place. What would have happened? Would he have allowed himself the physical closeness he craved at the end of his meeting with Cole?

But now, here in the company of his football friends, who dated girls every week and boasted about it, he became convinced he was just like them. He belonged with these men. The heated curiosity that Cole had awakened was eclipsed when he was with them and began to cool, if not completely, then to a slow simmer on a back burner.

In the fall, when his senior year in high school got underway, he thought about his future in college, now just under a year away. He had no strong calling to any particular profession. Throughout high school he had been good academically in all subjects, but had no love for any one specifically. Still, he thought he should have some goal or long-term plan for attending college.

"Practicing law is not glamorous," his father Jerry said, closing his laptop, when Lucas asked about the profession one evening. Jerry was sitting on the leather sofa in the living room, going over documents for a court case. "But it's a noble thing to do. Provide people with the legal recourses they are entitled to. Law is the structure by which society functions."

Lucas had been thinking about law, but also medicine, teaching, architecture — professions aunts and uncles and older cousins had pursued.

Rose overheard them from her seat in a red leather wing-back in a corner of the living room. She had a large picture book on Edvard Munch open on her lap. "Give yourself a chance, Lucas," she said as she looked up. "Get to college first, see what develops when you're there."

Lucas sat in an armchair opposite his father. "So, for example, if Coach Gomez acted unfairly when he suspended me, we could have used the law to make him let me play?"

Jerry cleared his throat. "It depends," he said slowly. "If he treated you differently than another student on the team that did something equally offensive, we might have had an argument." When he heard "offensive," Lucas felt a wounding in his chest, and he dropped his head and looked at the floor between his knees. "But then again," Jerry continued, looking away towards the window, "Coach Gomez could claim that he was preventing what he saw as immoral or indecent behavior, that he was enforcing school rules, and he would be within his rights."

Jerry got up and went to the bookshelf a few feet away, pulled out a book. He turned it and looked at it, hesitant, then gave it to Lucas. It was a copy of *The Trials of Oscar Wilde*. "This might shed some light on your question," Jerry said, and put his hand on Lucas's head and gave it a quick rub. "It's just food for thought. Society has rules."

Lucas looked at the cover and recognized with dismay the parallel his father was trying to make. His mouth and throat were like sand, and he got up and went into the kitchen to get some water. He overheard Rose ask Jerry what book he had selected, and his father's unintelligible response.

Lucas heard Rose say only, "Jerry," and he moved closer to the dining room, closer to the conversation.

"He's just confused, Rose," he heard his father say. "He's still young. He'll straighten out."

"He's too old to be just confused, Jerry. If he's different, we just have to accept it."

Lucas was disturbed that his mother again was thinking he was different than most men, and at the comparison his father had made. He wouldn't read the book. He knew Oscar Wilde was a prissy, flamboyant writer who had gone to prison for having an affair with a young man. Cole was Cole, but that was not who Lucas was, and he had no intention of being in that category. His father was right about the confused part. He didn't think he was different from his father in that regard, not the way his mother seemed to believe.

He remained in limbo about his future studies throughout his senior year in high school, getting excellent grades but enthusiastic only about football, which he saw as the venue for that confusion, a vestige of adolescence and male bonding that would not continue. Cole must have been an aberration, he decided, an unusually masculine gay man. He was afraid he would not be respectable in society, as his father was, if he allowed himself to be sexually active with other men, as he fantasized when he was alone in his room or in the shower. Coach Gomez had delivered that message loud and clear. He was not going to be like Oscar Wilde, which his father had used as an example of criminal behavior. He would have to ignore Rose's advice, which seemed to encourage him to do what he really felt like doing, date whom he wanted, not what others around him did or expected. She just didn't understand the insults and rejection he would have to endure if he followed her guidance.

He played his last scrimmage game in the spring, a few weeks before graduation. His team won the home game comfortably. Afterwards, in the showers, he looked around at his naked teammates slapping each other, spouting gulps of water like live statues in a surreal fountain, and realized this would be the last time they'd be together as a group, whether celebrating a victory or commiserating after a defeat. He had felt both exhilaration and shame for several years in the company of these young men, and now it was over. He tilted his head up to face the shower spray and closed his eyes tight, pretending that the wetness on his cheeks was all water.

Chapter 6

Rose Ascendant

Rose Tobin was born in Ireland in 1958, an only child. Her parents bundled her up in lace and boarded a cargo ship to New York in April of 1959, looking for better opportunities. Her uncle Garvan Tobin had preceded them by flying on a Boeing 707, one of the first jet-powered flights across the Atlantic, and had gotten a job selling medical supplies. He was single and thirty-two, and lived in an apartment in Greenwich Village.

In 1983 Rose turned twenty-four, and had already been a hospital nurse two years in Long Island, a crowded suburb of New York. Despite her parents' encouragement that she find an Irish boy from Queens, she was engaged to be married to Gerard Mann, a local attorney.

She had liked Jerry right away. Tall and solid, like a grandfather clock, he had green eyes and prematurely greying, tousled blond hair. Rose had pale, almost lavender skin, and her short black hair fell into place without any fussing on her part. Jerry had to bend down to kiss her at the end of that first evening, and she had pressed her breasts against him. In June of 1983, six months after their first date, they got engaged.

July first — the worst day of the year to be a patient in a hospital where interns deliver the first line of care, their first day as doctors after medical school. Rose was starting her shift in the ER, and Dr. Mandela introduced the new surgical intern to Rose.

"This is Miss Tobin," he said to the new doctor, Steve Stancil. "She's been here two years and she knows everything."

"Oh, no," Rose chuckled, shaking her head. "I don't think so." Her "o's" were short, the only trace of the brogue she had heard as a child.

"If I'm not around, and you have any questions, ask her," the senior doctor said.

Later that day Rose admitted a young woman with a deep cut on her forearm that required stitches. She made the patient lie down in a treatment bay, and went to get Dr. Stancil, the new intern.

The young doctor looked at the wound and looked up at Rose, who was standing next to him. She said nothing at first as he looked at the wound for a few seconds. His curly brown hair was humid and limp, and sweat was beginning to wet his forehead.

"I've already cleaned the wound up with peroxide. It's all set for suturing," she hinted at last to the doctor, breaking the trance he appeared to be in. "What sutures would you like, Doctor Stancil?" The patient was frowning, biting her lower lip.

"How about some three-o chromic catgut," Steve Stancil said, almost a question as he looked at her. She gave her head a quick little shake, closer to a vibration.

"Hmm," said Steve, looking at the patient. "On second thought, what's in the supply closet for this wound, Miss Tobin?"

Rose nodded and smiled. "Four-o nylon is what we have for that, doctor. I'll be right back with it, and some local anesthetic."

She made sure Steve had things under control before she left to help another nurse with a new patient, a pedestrian with mangled legs that was just being brought in. She could see, as she left, that Steve Stancil had good hands and was treating the wound gently. The patient's face was relaxed now, eyes closed.

Afterwards, Steve went to her when she was alone by the nurses' station.

"Thank you, Miss Tobin," he said. "I'll learn eventually."

"Nobody's born knowing. Call me Rose. You did a really nice job with that wound."

Steve blushed and walked away to the next patient.

Towards the end of Steve's month-long rotation in the ER, they were both at the weekly get-together at Vinnie's, a local bar. Rose liked Steve's easy smile, his unassuming interactions with both nurses and doctors. After a couple of beers, she found herself drawn to him, the first time she had been attracted to another man since being with Jerry. She wondered now if his deferential manner to her that first day, despite his medical degree, had endeared him to her. When Rose said good-night to the group, Steve followed her out. It was near midnight. In the parking lot she slowed down and waited for him to catch up.

"You're fun to be with," he said. "Is the evening over?"

"I think so."

"I'm finished in the ER as of tomorrow, so we won't be working together any more." He paused and raised his eyebrows before he spoke again. "Would you like to go out with me some time?"

"I'm engaged." She held up her ringed finger. "Not that you're not a nice looking guy." His brown, almond-shaped eyes caught the overhead lights of the parking lot, which also lit up his arched eyebrows.

Steve started to lean in as if to kiss her, but she put her hand on his chest and stopped him. He might be appealing, but she loved Jerry. She walked away to her car without saying good-night, eyes down.

The next day was Saturday, and she met Jerry at his apartment to go look for a place they might rent together. He wanted them to move in before the wedding, which still had no date. She looked around at the mess in his place — an old pizza box on the kitchen counter, empty cans of soda and beer on the table — and saw that once they lived together her life would become one of negotiating. But it would be worth it. He was like a fountain of inner calm and self-confidence, and yet she knew that in bed she could make him moan and thrash if she stuck her tongue in his ear. She liked having that power over a strapping, handsome man.

When she went to work in the ER the next day, she was told she was temporarily assigned to the surgical floor. When she got there, Steve Stancil was at the nurses' station working on patients' charts.

"You're here, not the ER?" He smiled when he saw her, showing his even, white teeth.

"For now," she said, and sighed. She liked the intensity of the ER.

"Nice."

At ten that evening, an hour before the end of her shift, she received a new patient. He was under arrest and had been assigned a private room so that the policeman guarding him would not alarm other patients. He had already undergone surgery to repair intestinal perforations from the gunshots the police had fired.

When she walked into the patient's room she was jarred by the sight of a policeman by the bed, the sleeping patient with one wrist handcuffed to the bed's side rail. She frowned at the sight.

The patient was a light-skinned, small black man in his late twenties with a worrisome pallor. The name on the chart was Ray Charlton, and he looked like a sleeping child to her, vulnerable, in need of care instead of restraint. The incongruity of his weakened, serious condition and the handcuffed wrist made her angry.

"Is this really necessary?" she barked at the cop as she rattled the handcuff against bed rail.

The cop, a middle-aged white man with grey short hair bristling out below his hat, scowled. "There's a court order," he spat out. "He's under arrest."

Rose shook her head, clenched her teeth, and took the patient's vitals. The man's eyelids fluttered but remained closed.

She rushed back to the nursing station, where Steve Stancil was still at the desk.

"Did you see Mr. Charlton in 323 yet?" she asked him.

"No. Why?"

"He's really pale. His pulse is fast, 125, and his blood pressure is only 90 over 60."

"Let me check the labs." Steve looked on the chart and saw the latest blood count from the recovery room, after the surgery. "The blood count was good two hours ago," he said, flipping through the chart.

"Can you just go take a look at him, please?" She tried to keep the annoyance out of her voice, but Steve's look of surprise told her she had failed.

"You're right. He looks like shit," Steve said when he hustled back into the nurses' station. He paged the operating surgeon. "This guy's crashing," he said on the phone. The surgeon came to the floor immediately and ordered x-rays. The CT scanner was new technology in the hospital, one of the first in the region, and too slow for an emergency like this.

While the patient was in the x-ray suite, the surgeon called the floor. "He's going back to the OR," the surgeon said to Rose on the phone. "Tell Dr. Stancil he made a good call. This guy is probably hemorrhaging internally."

Ray Charlton was in the hospital three weeks. Towards the end of his stay Rose went to his room so she could administer a medication. The cop, a different one now and more affable, waited out in the hall.

"I'll be glad to be out of here," Ray said, "although I'm going back to jail until my case is heard in court."

"What happened?" She drew the medication from the vial into a syringe. "Why did they arrest you?"

"I got busted for dealing. I lost my job at the tire place — you know Tyrone's?"

Rose nodded. "That's where I get my tires."

"I got laid off and I got three kids, you know?" he said. "And this dude at work says when I'm walking out my last day, 'Hey, you want to make some cash?' So I say, 'Sure.' Well, it was dealing, you know."

"What? Dealing what?"

"Pot, mostly, but also horse, some times."

She shook her head. "So how'd you get shot?"

"Cops saw me in the park, making a deal. Just some pot to a college kid." He shook his head and paused. "Stupid, you know? I ran, and when they yelled 'Stop' I just kept running. They shot me three times."

"You could've died." Rose said. He nodded and closed his eyes, which were starting to show a flow down his short but very curly black lashes. She pushed the medication into the IV, and she saw that Ray was breathing through his mouth now, eyes clenched in regret.

"Who's taking care of your kids?" She wrapped up her equipment to move on to the next patient.

"Their mother. She's a nurse's aide in a nursing home. She always worked the late shift so one of us always home for them, you know?" Ray let out a sob. "I don't know, now."

Later that day she went back into Ray Charlton's room to take his vitals and give him his afternoon medications. She saw that the cop was not near the room, evidently gone to the toilet, and Ray was not in his bed. She could hear water running in the bathroom through the closed door, and when she knocked, he said, "Coming," and then the door opened.

He was shaving, cheeks still covered in lather, his feet shackled. He was wearing his hospital gown backwards, with the opening to the front, and as he stood facing her the gown yawned open for an instant and she saw his genitals. They were the color of chocolate, much darker than the rest of his caramel skin, and she was surprised that this short, thin man had a phallus of that girth and length. She experienced a pleasurable contraction deep in her pelvis, which surprised and disturbed her. She had never felt this with a patient before, and she had seen plenty of handsome naked men in the hospital.

"I'll leave your medications at the bedside," she said. Her voice was hoarse. "Take them when you're done shaving." She kept her eyes on his face, not looking down, where she wanted to look. Ray had his gown secured now with his free hand, the one that wasn't holding the razor. He was not flirting. "I'll come back later for your vitals."

On Thursday, as she walked to her car in the parking lot, she saw Steve. He waved and went to her.

"I know you go to Vinnie's on Thursdays, but would you like to grab a bite with me instead?" He paused. "I know you're engaged, but just dinner? My kid sister wants to go into nursing. I want to pick your brain."

"How old is she?"

"Sixteen."

Rose didn't see a problem. She liked talking to him, and Jerry wasn't expecting her tonight. He had lots of paperwork to catch up on.

"Sure."

Dinner was at a small, dim trattoria. As they walked in, Rose could smell the cologne he was wearing, something she had smelled before but couldn't place. Over pizza and salad they talked shop, movies, and nursing education, all relaxed and flowing. They had seen the same movies, and their tastes were similar in music too. Steve paid the bill, declining Rose's offer to split it. "You did me the favor," he said.

Outside in the parking lot, Steve put his arm on her forearm. "Thank you," he said.

"Oh, no, don't mention it. It was fun." She could still detect the fragrance he was wearing, and didn't move her arm away from his touch. She realized suddenly that his cologne was the same her uncle Garvan had worn. He had died suddenly last year. The sadness of losing her funny, handsome uncle caused her to slump her shoulders, and she looked at the cleft in Steve's chin. It reminded her of Uncle Garvan's.

Steve stepped to her and put his arms around her in a loose embrace. She was comforted by the fragrance, and she rested her head on his shoulder. She couldn't understand why she was doing this. She would have preferred Jerry, but when Steve kissed her and asked her to follow him in her car to his apartment, she nodded.

She thought about what she was doing as she followed him, and once or twice considered turning around, go to her own place. She suspected, as they began to get close on his bed in the small but neat bedroom, that the sight of the patient's genitals the night before had awakened a compelling need that was being filled now, and which Jerry had been too busy and tired to meet recently. Afterwards, instead of just the guilt she was expecting, she felt a tenderness for Steve. She liked his gentleness, his lilting voice, his comfort with his own unremarkable, even soft, body.

At work the next day, she was relieved when Steve acted as if nothing had happened. There was no inappropriate familiarity, nothing even close to intimacy. She looked forward to seeing Jerry that night.

A few days later, on her first evening back in the ER, a major multiple trauma was brought in by ambulance. A moribund fifteen-year-old girl had been a passenger in a car driven by her intoxicated seventeen-year-old boyfriend, who had died at the scene. The pretty, chubby teen had a feeble pulse and no blood pressure. She was in a fancy dress, wearing green eyeshadow and pink lipstick. Rose passed a nasogastric tube into the stomach while the doctor examined her. When Rose got the tube into the stomach, pink fluid poured out into a waiting basin. The reek of sweet wine hit Rose hard, and two pints poured out before she had even attached it to a suction machine.

The doctor examined the girl's arms and legs, tested reflexes. "Spinal cord injury. Paralyzed from the neck down — if she survives."

When the girl was stabilized, Rose and another nurse wheeled the stretcher towards the ICU. Steve was there doing a lung puncture. She knew the patient was in good hands, and felt a smug privilege that she had witnessed his early struggles in the ER, and maybe had had a small hand in refining his skills. He finished the procedure and followed Rose out to the elevator.

"Can I see you again?" They were out of earshot of the other nurses.

She saw a deep need there, almost a desperation, and she jabbed the down button for the elevator repeatedly.

"I can't," she said in a hoarse whisper. "That was a one-time thing. For whatever reason, it happened."

His thin lips were in that grimace she had seen that first day. "Please. I just need to talk. I promise."

The elevator doors opened. She walked in, pushed the "open" button. There was something there she wanted to respond to.

"One more meeting," she said. The elevator buzzed in protest on being held open. "To talk." She let go of the button.

"My place tomorrow night at ten." There was a smile on his face now. "I'll make some snacks." The elevator door closed before she could object to going to his apartment. But she told herself that there would be no risk of another sexual encounter.

Steve was wearing a blue tee-shirt, jeans, and sandals when she got to his place. The brown curls that covered his head were still wet from a shower. He brought out glasses and a bottle of sauvignon blanc.

"So what did you want to talk about?" Rose asked as she sipped her wine.

"This is difficult for me." He took a big gulp of his own glass.

Rose waited.

"Okay. I know I'm older than you, twenty-nine. But the fact is that you're only the second woman I've ever had sex with."

Rose saw that he was watching her, and gave him all her attention. "So?"

"I was very inexperienced. I thought you would notice."

"You were fine," she said. "Better than just fine." Immediately she was sorry she had said it.

"Really?" He held his wine glass with both hands.

"Really."

"Good. That's a relief. I wasn't sure."

"You've never had a girlfriend?"

He shook his head. "No. I haven't even dated much. I don't think women find me attractive."

"You're a nice-looking man, and very sweet. Women like that."

He smiled, but said nothing.

After a minute, she stood up. "I should go."

"Thank you," he said as they stood by the front door. "You've been wonderful to me." He paused and looked at the floor, as if he didn't want to meet her eyes when he said, "You're a really good person."

She couldn't remember anybody saying that to her before, and she was caught off guard. Her parents held on to the way of communicating from the old country: compliments were not even hinted at. Jerry was enthusiastic about life, and affectionate, but he never praised her, as if unaware that she had any good qualities. He never thanked her for cleaning up his apartment, or for making dinner and leaving the kitchen spotless, as if it was something that he expected of her. She saw real appreciation in Steve's face. Despite his intelligence and education he seemed helpless to her, like a lost child. She kissed him on the cheek, and he put his arms around her. Soon their faces turned to each other.

In bed a few minutes later, naked and uncovered by sheets, they kissed as he lay on top, inside her. His self-confidence was greater now than during their first time, his movements more assured. He found her right hand with his left and brought it up to his face, licked her middle finger, and brought her hand down to his buttocks. With his other hand he pulled one buttock away from the other, and placed her finger on his anus. He moved swiftly, and she allowed it to happen, too wrapped up in the moment to pull away from this unspoken and unexpected request. She felt the moist, silk-like texture underneath her finger, and pressed down on it. Then he put both his hands on her breasts, and as he climaxed she felt the sphincter beneath her finger contract in synchrony with his pulsations inside her.

Afterwards, they lay in silence in the dim light of a floor lamp.

"You said I'm the second woman you've ever been with." She sat up and wiped her finger with a tissue from the night-stand. "Have you ever been with men?"

Steve hesitated. "No." He paused. "Although I've thought about it," he mumbled. He sat up and turned, swinging his feet to the floor on his side of the bed, so all she saw was his pale, glistening back. "But now, with this gay-related immune deficiency that we're starting to call AIDS…"

"So I was just a substitute for what you really wanted?" She was a little insulted by the possibility, but she was also curious.

"No, of course not." Steve picked his underwear off the floor and stood up to put it on before turning to look at her. "If I hadn't been attracted to you, we wouldn't be here."

"I've never had a man who wanted me to do that before," she said as she got up to go to the bathroom.

"Well," he hesitated. "It *is* an erogenous part of the body."

Afterwards, they dressed in silence after she washed in the bathroom. At the front door, they looked at each other before she exited. His eyebrows were high on his forehead again. They didn't kiss. Rose smiled, put her hand on his arm and gave his biceps three quick pats of friendship, a resetting of the relationship.

As she drove home in the dark, the roads mostly empty, she thought about Uncle Garvan. She missed him, his optimism, his jokes, which could erupt rapid-fire. How she wished she had known him better, had known about his being gay. All she had known with certainty was that he was fairly religious, and went to mass every Sunday. But the details about his plans for vacations, friendships, his romantic life, had been off-limits. She wondered, had he had a boyfriend? The big secret about his basic nature had brought with it a barrier to a greater emotional connection.

She had loved his Irish looks, tall and thin, like a six-foot bamboo cane, but with round, red cheeks and eyes that were like blue flames from a stove. After several bouts of feverish illness that had started last year ("Oh, it's just the flu again," he had said to Rose on the phone), he went into St. Vincent's Hospital in Greenwich Village, his own neighborhood. Neither Rose nor her parents had known about the hospitalization. He listed his brother, her father, as next-of-kin, and the hospital called her parents' home early one morning to say that he was terminal. Rose met her father at the bedside.

Garvan's room was in a separate isolation ward. She thought she might be in the wrong part of the hospital. As she walked down the hall she saw room after room of young men, cachectic with impending death, many of them with the black-purple splotches of Kaposi's sarcoma on their arms and faces, and she suddenly understood their diagnosis, and why they were all in one section. She had never seen anything like this back in the hospital in Hempstead, where AIDS had rarely been diagnosed, and was horrified at the sight of these dying, handsome men. Every room had IV poles with bags and bags of fluids either being infused or standing by. Garvan being here seemed like a mistake.

Rose and her father were met at the bedside by his doctor, a short, greying man in his fifties, about Garvan's age. In bed, covered by sheets and blankets, her uncle was pale and unconscious. A purple cancer the size of a child's hand covered the left side of his neck. He had worn a scarf the last time she had seen him, even though it was summer.

"It's not good news, I'm afraid," Dr. Braun said in a German accent.

"But what is wrong, doctor, that he is dying so fast?" Rose had never heard her father's brogue quite this thick.

"He has AIDS." The doctor paused, and looked at their faces. "We know this illness occurs almost exclusively in gay men, although he has never admitted to anyone here that he had sex with other men."

Rose nodded. So that was the secrecy.

"But he just isn't married, doctor," her father said. "That's all, he just isn't married. Are you sure that's what's wrong, now?"

The doctor nodded. "It's a classic case of it, and the blood tests are unequivocal."

"But he wouldn't have done anything immoral, doctor." Her father's voice was trembling. "He's a good Catholic. It's not as if he did something that God wanted to punish, like those other men you just mentioned. He doesn't deserve this."

Rose saw that the doctor closed his face to her father and stayed silent. She thought of putting her hand around her father's waist, but did not. It was not something they did in this family. She could see him swaying, and said, "Why don't you go to the lounge down the hall and rest a few minutes? I'll come get you soon."

After her father had gone, Rose said, "Have you seen many of these cases here?" She had never seen any in the hospital in Hempstead, those rare patients held in isolation in separate wards, and many nurses and doctors had been afraid of having contact with them.

"Oh, yes," Dr. Braun said. "Our first case here was almost four years ago."

Rose shook her head. "I hope you understand, it's hard for my father to accept what you said about his brother's sex life. My uncle was so religious."

The doctor hesitated. "As it happens, our very first case in this hospital was a Catholic priest transferred here from a hospital in Philadelphia." He looked at Garvan and shook his head.

"How long does he have?" She leaned against the footboard of Garvan's bed. Her beloved uncle. She wanted to hug him, but she was unsure how risky it might be for her if she touched him, and she was too ashamed of being thought ignorant by the doctor if she asked. All she could do was lean her hips against his bed. Her back and her feet were hurting, although she had worn comfortable shoes and it was still morning.

"Not long, unfortunately," the doctor said. "The pneumonia is very extensive and not responding to the antibiotics. A few hours, perhaps."

"Has he received his last rites?" She knew that Garvan would want them, although she did not believe.

"Oh, yes. Late last night. He requested them before he went into a coma."

Rose went to the lounge to look for her father, and they went back to Garvan's room. They stood side by side at the foot of the bed. After a few minutes she wanted to get something to eat in the cafeteria and give her father a break from the deathwatch. When she looked at him, she saw that he was looking at his brother with abysmal grief, close to losing the struggle with sobbing. Unable to speak without losing control, she bit her lower lip and remained silent. At that moment, Garvan's breathing became irregular and rhonchial, and he died less than a minute later as they watched. Rose was stunned, incredulous that her uncle was gone, and couldn't bring herself to hold her father, who was helpless with weeping. Her hands instead went to her face and covered it.

On her way to Jerry's place from her own apartment, the day after seeing Steve for the last time, Rose stopped for groceries. She would make a good dinner for Jerry.

She cooked pasta with sausage and kale, and it was only as they were sitting down to it that she realized that it had been Garvan's favorite dish.

"You look so sad, Rose. Is something wrong?"

She looked down at her plate, and remembered how inadequate she had felt at Garvan's bedside the day he died, not hugging her uncle, and not able to comfort her father. She looked at Jerry and shrugged, scrunched her eyes to prevent the wetness from escaping them. Jerry got up from the table, went to her and pulled her up to standing. His arms went around her, comforting wings. She couldn't wait to marry him.

When they went to bed after she cleaned up the kitchen, he turned to her and rested his hand on her arm, already drowsy from the long work day. She yanked him to her. She wanted to swallow him, become one with him. When he moved over her, and was inside, she felt that she was erasing her infidelity, an insignificant misstep. More than anything, she wanted to give Jerry the utmost pleasure, and she licked her middle finger and placed it between his buttocks. As her finger moved deeper into the crevice Jerry stopped.

"What are you doing?" he asked.

"It's supposed to feel good. You want to try?"

"Nope." He took her hand and moved it away. "Thanks for the offer, though," in a tone he might have used if she had offered him dogfood.

Rose broke into a hoarse, throaty laugh, and they continued their lovemaking and finished in the familiar, comforting way. The release was like ice cream.

In the dark, while Jerry slept, she saw moonlight through the space in the blinds. The silver, furtive light made her think of Garvan again, and she felt a vast, engulfing sadness at the injustice that had ruled his life.

Chapter 7

Craig and Cassandra

On a Saturday in late April, two months before his high school graduation, Lucas was helping Rose put groceries away.

"I have this new part-time assistant at the gallery. His name is Craig. Young man, your age."

"Oh?" Lucas said as he put canned goods in the pantry.

"He's going to Bard College in the fall, to study music. I don't think it's far from Vassar."

"A half hour, I think."

"He's really smart, so nice, and so sophisticated. Maybe you can stop by the gallery later today? I'll introduce you."

Lucas looked at her, gave a small shrug. "Sure."

Craig was a short, thin waif of a man who plucked his eyebrows. He wore skin-tight pants and a flowered shirt, and his handshake felt to Lucas as if he was holding a dead fish.

"Isn't the light in this Hopper amazing?" Craig asked as they stood side by side. All Lucas could see was a dark painting of an old house with green windows and a brown roof.

"I don't see any people," he said. He thought it was a dull, depressing painting.

Craig laughed and showed him another painting a few feet away. It was by Egon Schiele, and it depicted a man wearing only briefs, one arm raised, a huge muff of hair in the armpit. Lucas was intrigued by the suggestiveness of the image, but thought it was crude and unfinished.

"Hmm," he said.

Afterwards, when Rose got home and they were in the kitchen, Lucas said, "Why did you think I'd have anything in common with that guy, mom?" His tone was controlled, but the annoyance was there.

Rose looked surprised. "Well. I just thought you might at least get acquainted. You know, have a friend or something already up in the Hudson Valley."

He shook his head and didn't look at her. "It's okay Mom. I'll be all right without your help." He went to his room and closed the door louder than was necessary. He was annoyed that Rose was trying to make friends for him, intruding into his social life, with someone like Craig. How could she think someone who was a caricature of a pansy would be someone he'd interested in?

He dated a few women during that last year in high school, partially spurred by his wish to still Rose's efforts and curiosity. He never even attempted anything sexual with them, and went out with them not just because of Rose, but because his male friends, mostly members of the football team, talked about going out with women frequently. Dating was obviously the thing to do, but he never felt the urge to be physical with the girls, and he went out only once or twice with any of them.

A few weeks after the Craig incident, they were at the dinner table talking about colleges and Lucas's final decision to go to Vassar. He had liked the campus, the professors he had met. It had a welcoming, relaxed feel to it. The other schools, especially Columbia and NYU, had seemed huge and impersonal.

"Vassar is beautiful," Rose said to Jerry. "Wait till you see it."

"I'll make sure to go with you on registration day," Jerry said.

"It's so exciting to be going to college. You know Georgette, from the gallery?" Rose said. "She brought her daughter in today, Cassandra. A beautiful girl. She's going to NYU in the fall but she'll be working with us on Saturdays until then."

"I really didn't like NYU. I'm glad I'm going to Vassar," said Lucas.

"Hmm," Jerry said, cocking his head at Rose. "Cassandra's beautiful, huh?"

Rose nodded, keeping her eyes down on her bowl of ice cream. "She is," she said, with no emphasis.

Lucas's eyebrows went up and he suppressed an eye roll, but he remained silent as he finished his dessert.

"Why don't you go meet her, Lucas? She must be your age." Jerry said, putting his spoon down.

"Dad, come on. I don't even know her."

"I think I'll go make some coffee," Rose said as she got up and started to clear the dishes.

"Where does she go to school now?" Lucas asked Rose, turning his head away from his father. "I don't remember any Cassandras from school."

"She's graduating from Mount Saint Mary, across town. It's a good school," Rose said from the kitchen.

"We won't hold the Catholic thing against her," Jerry said with a smile.

Theirs was not a religious family, although Rose had been brought up Catholic and Jerry Lutheran. That familial background had been swept aside because both Rose and Jerry found most religions full of hypocrisy and had never exposed Lucas to any of them. As a result, Lucas just had an intellectual interest in religion, as he did for many philosophies.

Jerry continued to encourage Lucas to meet Cassandra like an audio tape gone berserk on replay while they all cleared dishes.

Rose remained silent, although Lucas saw that her mouth was tense and that she kept giving Jerry brief, hard stares. Finally she said, "Jerry, he'll go out with her if he wants to. He's old enough to know what he wants."

Lucas was embarrassed. He wanted to relieve Rose of the burden of protecting him and censoring Jerry, but didn't see how to do that. His mother seemed to understand him to a degree with which made him uncomfortable, as if she could see his reluctance to go meet this girl projected on his forehead. When Lucas relented and agreed to go to the gallery, Rose looked at him and said nothing. The smile on Jerry's face looked like he would click his heels if he stood up.

Cassandra was indeed beautiful, with long, chestnut hair that reflected the lights in the gallery with golden shimmers. "Hi, Lucas," she said when they were introduced, smiling and tilting her head to the side, charming, solicitous. Her smile showed small and even alabaster teeth, and she was conversant and outgoing. He was charmed, but felt zero chemistry. Still, he asked her to go to the movies, more because it was expected, if not by his mother, then perhaps by Georgette and Cassandra, as well as, of course, Jerry. Lucas also thought that this beautiful, quiet girl may indeed prove to be someone for whom he could come to feel some form of attraction that would be acceptable to him and to society at large.

On their afternoon date the following Saturday, she walked close to him on the way to the movie theater, and kept glancing at him. She let her hand brush his a couple of times, but Lucas limited the touching to putting his hand around her waist as they entered the theater. They were seeing *The Hours*, a film adaption of a recent novel based on Virginia Woolf's *Mrs. Dalloway*. Lucas had read and been mesmerized by the contemporary novel, then had sought out Woolf's work and found it plodding in comparison. He did not try to hold hands with Cassandra during the movie.

On their two subsequent dates, also to afternoon movies, he felt nothing and went no further with her physically.

Cassandra took his arm on their way home on the third and what would be their final date. As he dropped her off at her apartment building he realized that they had never had anything to talk about, other than the movies they had seen in a casual, non-passionate way. He had been close to bored on their dates, although she had remained vivacious and talkative. He saw plainly that she was a perfect girl, not just beautiful, but intelligent, outgoing, considerate. She was like a perfectly splendid sofa for which he had no use. This would be it, he decided, despite her wonderful qualities and the imprimatur of conformity and cachet that being with her bestowed upon him. She was smiling radiantly at him, clearly having enjoyed their time together, and he felt a great rush of regard for her as they said good-bye on the sidewalk, a few feet from the canopied entrance of her building. At that moment, on the brink of the date coming to its conclusion, he wondered whether perhaps he could nurture that feeling of appreciation into something like sexual attraction. Maybe that's how other men did it, how he was supposed to approach a relationship with a woman. He leaned in as if to kiss her, and she closed her eyes and tilted her head up. Lucas kept his eyes open as he kissed her on the cheek, and kept his hands off her.

"I've had a nice time with you," Lucas said. He hoped she understood that it was over without the unpleasantness of an outright good-bye.

But Cassandra nodded and said, "And I've really enjoyed myself going out with you." She smiled, expectant. When he said nothing, she said, "Do you want to see me again?"

Lucas was overcome by her vulnerability and sincerity, and almost choked on his saliva when he tried to speak. He cleared his throat. "I'll be going away to school in the fall. Is there any point?" he finally said. He ignored what he knew: that his friends had formed relationships they planned to maintain when they went away to college.

Cassandra looked into his eyes and did not smile. She nodded her perfect head, turned, and walked into her building. Lucas felt a devastating inadequacy and a maddening guilt as he rushed home, as if he had just stepped on a kitten. He wondered, as he crossed an aggressively busy Columbus Avenue, whether being hit by a speeding truck would be an agonizing and incomplete erasure, or a certain, instant death.

Jerry and Rose drove him to Vassar on registration day that fall, the car loaded with boxes of clothes and a new microwave. "Gorgeous," Rose said, almost to herself, when she saw the campus again. "Absolutely gorgeous."

"A lot of history here. I've researched it," Jerry said as he and Lucas carried boxes into the dorm, passing young men and women doing the same in the halls and stairs. "I'll bet you're going to have a good time."

After Lucas had settled in his dorm room, they walked around the campus on the tree-lined lanes and on walks paved with bluestone.

"It's beautiful here — the buildings, the students," said Rose as they neared the parking lot where they had left their car. "I've never seen so many gorgeous men and women. Lots of opportunities for a great social life."

"He's here to study, Rose," Jerry said, putting his arm around Lucas's shoulders. He leaned in and smelled his father's spicy deodorant, and saw that this clumsy man he loved so much was about to cry.

"Time for you guys to go." Lucas hugged them as they stood next to the Volvo. Rose's eyes were starting to well up. He couldn't imagine not having her in his life every day, the way she had been up to now, cheering him on all his life. "It's only an hour-plus train ride into Grand Central, Mom," he said, although he was addressing himself as well as his father, because he saw that although Jerry's eyes were still dry, his eyebrows were knitting furiously.

He stepped away from them and from the Volvo and watched as they got in and the car moved away, Rose waving, trying to smile. He looked around at the other students going in and out of the dorm. Nobody seemed to pay the slightest attention to him, and he knew no one.

Chapter 8

Angela and Vassar

Lucas declared philosophy as his major, and he met Angie the first week of school in his Eastern Philosophy study group. They were sitting in a circle on folding chairs in a small classroom, and she was the most vocal of the twelve students. She laughed when Lucas asked the instructor what role exercise, specifically yoga, played in Eastern religions.

"Yoga as we do it here is mostly a Western invention," she said before the instructor could even begin to answer. "A German woman studied yoga meditation in India and created the exercises that we now practice here."

Angie held her gaze on him as she spoke. Her large brown eyes sparkled, and her long, even teeth gleamed as she spoke with complete confidence, not even bothering to look at the instructor for approval. He wished he could be that certain about things, that self-confident. She was still wearing cut-offs even though the glow of summer was fading, and her symmetrical, angular face had no make-up.

Afterwards, as they exited the Federalist yellow brick building where the class had met, she made it a point to walk next to him as they descended the stairs from the portico.

"Why were you so curious about exercise and Eastern religions? she asked. They stood at the base of the stairs, on a lane flanked by oaks. A breeze caught her auburn hair and blew it across her face.

"It's important to me. Physical fitness. I played a lot of football in high school."

"I could tell," she said, squeezing his rounded biceps in her little hand. "No puff ball, you."

"You're in good shape too," he said, but didn't touch her, although he knew he could have. He knew she would have let him do a mock squeezing of her own well-muscled arm, would have welcomed his making a move.

"I happen to teach yoga part time," she said. "That's why I spouted off like that. If you're interested, I can show you some basic positions and what the spiritual connection is." And then she gave a little laugh. "Supposedly."

He felt awkward not saying yes, although he didn't have much interest in yoga. And even though he could see she was pretty, he was not particularly moved to respond to her. Still, he said, "Sounds great," because it seemed like the thing to do, and he didn't know how to say no without seeming rude. A cool breeze blew suddenly, and he got goose bumps. The oaks nearby lost some of the yellowing September leaves. She gave him her address, just off campus, and they agreed to meet the next afternoon.

He had been thinking about Cole since he had arrived at Vassar, had been hoping to run into him. He looked up the telephone number of the hotel he had stayed in with his mother over a year ago. When he was connected to reception, a female voice told him that Cole no longer worked there. "Did he go back to school at Vassar?" Lucas asked. She didn't know, she said. She hadn't seen him for several months. "You don't know his last name, by any chance?" he asked, and she did not. He wished he had learned his last name that evening. Vassar was a big place, and it was not likely that he would run into him. He did not sleep well that night.

The next day, after his last class, he walked the four blocks to the address Angie had given him. When he got there, she greeted him at the door dressed in black tights that delineated her genitals. "Glad you made it. I wasn't sure you were going to come."

"Oh, no. I'm here. I even brought work-out clothes." He showed her his gym bag.

There were empty Coke cans and bags of snacks strewn about the living room. She showed him the bathroom. When he came out in the shorts and tee shirt he had brought, Angie unrolled two exercise mats after she cleared some of the clutter in the living room. "I have two messy roommates," she said. She placed her hands on his chest and abdomen, under his tee shirt, to demonstrate the rhythm of breaths. Lucas felt a movement in his genitals, a contraction, when he felt her smooth hands on him.

They started with basic moves. Her hands lingered over his bare thighs below his shorts when she corrected his positions. She did this repeatedly, and he started to become aroused. "Your leg hair is like fleece," she said as she brushed it gently with the palm of her hand. No one had ever touched him so deliberately and so intimately. As he stood doing warrior II, she put her hands deep inside the sleeves of his tee shirt, holding him under his arms to help twist his chest. The feel of her hands in his armpits caused him to feel another, more energetic stirring in his pelvis. Later, when he was trying to do down dog, she placed one hand on the backs of his muscle-bound thighs near his buttocks, and the other hand underneath, on his pubis just above his genitals, to raise his hips. When he stood up straight, his black nylon shorts were tented by his erection. She kissed him, pressed herself against him, and led him to her bedroom.

She undressed first, dropping her tank top and tights on the floor as he stood and watched, paralyzed. His throat felt dry and constricted when he saw her body, muscular and beautiful. It was the first time he had seen a naked woman. He spoke with a squeaky croak. "I've never done this before," he said. Immediately he regretted the confession. He could have forged ahead and done what he had to do without her knowing he was a virgin.

Angie moved up to him and hugged him as she kissed him, then took his clothes off. "It's okay," she said. Then she took him to her bed.

The sensations he felt that afternoon were not like anything he had experienced before. The warmth and closeness of another person, the receipt of pleasure and the giving of it, and the fact that this beautiful woman was bringing him to orgasm were things he could not have imagined during all the years he had brought sexual pleasure to himself.

The next few weeks and months were the happiest of his life. In later years he would look upon them and think of himself as having been conveniently delusional. But for now, the feeling that he at last belonged in the world, just like his high school friends, was overwhelmingly reassuring, and he forgot his attraction for men.

He learned to relax with her and become sexually playful. He let his erect member rub her genitalia gently without entering her for a few minutes, until she would wrap her legs around his waist, grab his buttocks, and push him in urgently. Or he would use his morning erection while she was still asleep, place it between her thighs from behind until she began to awaken and moved against him.

A year later, having enjoyed frequent sex and warm companionship, and feeling now that he had at last left his adolescent cravings behind, he agreed when she proposed that they move in together into a tiny apartment. Rose sounded incredulous and almost shrill when he told her on the phone that he'd be moving out of the dorm to live with her. "What's this?" she exclaimed. "I didn't even know you had a girlfriend."

"We've been together for a year. Her name is Angie."

"I had no idea. No idea," Rose said. "Are you sure about this?"

"We're just going to live together, mom."

Rose held silence for a second or two, then said, "Wait till I tell your father. He'll be so happy." But her voice was flat, joyless, and Lucas was expecting more enthusiasm than he heard. "I've got to go. I've got something on the stove."

Soon after that he went home for a weekend. Angie stayed on campus.

"So tell us about Angie," Jerry said as they sat down to dinner. Rose had redecorated the small dining room. The heavy dark green drapes he had looked at during the conversation about Oscar Wilde with his father were gone. In their place were yellow sheers that even with the Manhattan skyline glittering in the darkness gave the room a sunny look.

Lucas hesitated. "She's very nice. She's studying business administration and sociology."

Jerry looked at Lucas with anticipation. Lucas shrugged. "You guys will meet her some time." Rose looked at him with a furrow between her eyebrows. He wished she were smiling, as his father was.

"I'm thinking of going into law after all, dad," he said at the end of dinner, while they were still at the table.

Rose started clearing dishes and walked back and forth to the kitchen, a few feet away. "You sure that's what you want?" she asked through the open pass-through.

Jerry put his elbows on the table, leaned forward. "What made you decide?"

"I think all the philosophy courses I've taken did it." Lucas got up and helped Rose. "I really like philosophy but don't see a way of making a living at it. Law uses rational thinking, and deals with the human condition, much like philosophy, no?"

"I must say, that's certainly novel." He smiled and got up to put his arms around Lucas, whose hands were busy carrying plates and serving dishes.

Rose was running the water in the sink, and shouted over the noise, "I just want to make sure it's what you really want, not the path of least resistance."

"It's what he wants, honey," Jerry said as he helped Lucas clear dishes from the table. "It's what he wants."

"Yeah, well," he heard his mother utter under her breath, "I'm not sure he knows *what* he wants."

Lucas rinsed his hands in the sink as Rose stepped aside for him with an exaggerated distance, eyebrows halfway up her forehead, then he returned to the table to join Jerry for coffee. "And Angie's dad is a professor of criminal law at Rutgers. If he writes me a letter of recommendation, I'm likely to get into at least one of the law schools in New York."

"Have you even met her father?" Rose asked, frowning again as she poured the coffee.

"Not yet. We're going to visit her parents in New Jersey next month."

"This seems a little sudden to me," Rose mumbled as she sat down, looking at her hands wrapped around the hot mug.

Lucas led the voyage by mass transit to Maplewood, where Angie's parents lived. Having grown up in New Jersey, she was more comfortable behind the wheel of a car than on subways and trains. Her mother Olivia was about as tall as Angie, just above Lucas' jaw. She met them at the train station and hugged an unsmiling Angie, who kept her arms at her side and didn't hug back. Olivia extended her hand to shake Lucas'. Her hair was colored lighter than Angie's auburn, and cropped very short. They got into a new black Mercedes sedan that already had badly scratched bumpers. With Olivia behind the wheel, they crawled half a mile through empty streets to a two-story house with green siding. Inside, Olivia led them through a spacious and bright living room filled with oak and chestnut furniture. Angie disappeared, without a word, through sliding glass doors to the garden beyond, and Olivia took Lucas up a curving staircase to a guest bedroom on the second floor.

"Come down to the kitchen after you've settled in and we'll have lunch." Olivia smiled as she closed the door.

He looked around the room, bigger than his in his parents' apartment. The walls were powder blue, with matching curtains and bedspread. He had a strong sense of disquiet and was glad he would be spending only one night.

The three of them had lunch in the huge kitchen, which had an island as big as a twin bed and copper pots hanging on the walls. Olivia had made an elaborate chicken salad, which

Lucas complimented repeatedly. He noticed that Angie didn't talk to her mother, and addressed all her comments to him.

"What's your favorite class, Angie?" Olivia asked, leaning forward in her chair and putting her elbows on the table.

"They're all okay. Would you like more bread, Lucas?" Angie looked at him without even picking up the bread basket.

Andrew, Angie's father, came in from golf after lunch. He was tall and wiry, in his fifties, much older than Lucas would have anticipated. Angie did not hug her father. She allowed him to kiss her cheek, then skittered away and up the stairs to her room.

After introductions, he invited Lucas to the backyard. They sat in teak chairs having beers. Olivia had wheedled Angie into going shopping for new clothes for school, and they had gone off. Andrew asked Lucas about his plans to go to law school.

"Angie told us you're interested in becoming an attorney. Why do you want to go into law?" Andrew said. His bald head was shaved completely and gleamed in the autumn sun.

Lucas talked about being inspired by his philosophy courses and by his father's statement that law is the foundation of societies. As he spoke at some length, he saw that Andrew scowled, and his posture changed from a comfortable, lean-ing-back slouch to an upright, ready-to-jump-up one, like a coiled snake ready to strike.

"I must say, you have a musical voice for a man. Not an asset for an attorney. Not for litigation, anyway."

Lucas noticed a tightness around the man's mouth that was new. Andrew finished his beer, put the empty bottle down on the patio's slate floor next to his chair, and looked at the tree tops for so long Lucas thought he might have forgotten he was there.

"Angie says you two have been together for a year," he said finally. "How serious are you?" He was looking at Lucas out of the corners of his grey eyes, his face still turned up at the sky.

"We haven't talked marriage or anything like that," Lucas said, putting his half empty bottle on the floor. He was suddenly intensely uncomfortable, didn't want any more beer or chips, wanted to go as far from this house as possible. "But we spend all our time together when we're not in class." He sat up straight in his chair, looking around for a reason to get up and move away.

Andrew leaned back in his chair and clasped his hands behind his head, looking up at scattered clouds below a hazy sky. The steel frames of his glasses sparked in the dim sunlight. "How many women have you been with before Angie? How many girlfriends have you had, roughly?"

Lucas hesitated, reluctant to answer truthfully. He didn't see that this was any of this man's business. "None before Angie, actually." His mouth was dry, but he didn't want the warm beer.

Andrew nodded. "I didn't think so," he muttered. After a minute he said, not looking at him, eyes still squinting at the sky, "You want a letter of recommendation from me? That's what Angie said."

"It was her idea. It'd be nice, yes, but you don't really know me yet," Lucas said.

"First thing you've said that makes sense," Andrew said, getting up. "We'll see." He was not quite as tall as Lucas, but had perfect posture, and he was the most intimidating man Lucas had ever met. He went into the kitchen and left Lucas alone.

The rest of the weekend was tense for Lucas, and he looked only to Olivia for polite conversation at the dinner table, because even Angie appeared tightly wound. Andrew did not seek Lucas out again. Angie's interactions with both her parents remained restrained, laconic, a side of Angie he had not seen. Andrew was not at breakfast the next morning before they went back to Vassar. Lucas didn't see Angie say good-by to her father, and she thanked her mother for driving them to the train station without giving her a hug.

"Was there something going on with your dad?" Lucas asked Angie on the train.

She shrugged. "I'm not sure what you mean."

"He seemed okay at first when I met him, but he seemed to get annoyed at something while we were talking, and he stayed that way."

"He's a damn grouch. I didn't see anything unusual, I hate to tell you."

He considered first before he brought it up. "You didn't talk to either one of your parents much." He wasn't sure he should be butting into Angie's family dynamics, wasn't sure he wasn't being presumptuous.

She looked at him, seemed to consider speaking, but hesitated. "Something happened years ago. It's over now. I'll tell you some day."

Lucas nodded. "Okay."

Maybe he had been wrong about Andrew not liking him. Maybe it all had to do with Angie.

Andrew and Olivia visited Vassar to see Angie a few times later that academic year.

"Ladies, this young man and I are going to a bar for some beers," Andrew announced right after lunch their first visit. Lucas was relieved that Andrew appeared to be making a friendly gesture. He had been dreading seeing the man again after his visit to their home in New Jersey, but Angie pulled Lucas aside and convinced him when he hesitated.

"He wants to see if you have any talent for law, and a letter of recommendation from him will open doors for you," she said.

In the bar, Andrew explained points of criminal law, and then drilled Lucas, questioning his reasoning. Andrew was unsmiling, assuming a hostile tone for that hour in the bar. These sessions occurred the next two times they visited, over the course of the semester.

On his third and final session with Andrew at a pub near the college, Lucas felt more intimidated than before by Andrew's manner, drilling him about principles of law, punctilious and unsmiling. Lucas sweated through his shirt during their last few minutes together in the pub.

"You look like you swam across the Hudson," Angie said to him when she saw him afterwards.

"Yeah, well. He's a tough cookie, your dad."

She went up to him and kissed him. "Don't let him get to you. He can be a pain in the butt. But he must like you if he's even bothering to pursue it with you. And remember, a good letter from him will mean a lot to a law school admissions committee."

Lucas did not tell her about the final moments of their conversation. Andrew had stopped asking Lucas about points of law and went silent for a few minutes while he looked at his half-empty beer stein. When he looked up at Lucas, his grey eyes were shards of shale. "What do you want with my daughter?"

It was not a question Lucas was expecting. "I — we love each other. We like to be together."

Andrew shook his head. "I don't believe you really love her, but I can see my daughter loves you. I know the likes of you. You don't fool me."

Lucas's throat tightened. He was outraged at the accusation, which he didn't even understand, and he could not have made any sounds, even if he had wanted to. He coughed into his paper napkin. Andrew paid the bill and left, Lucas trailing after him to the parking lot.

The exchange tortured Lucas. Andrew remained silent in the car going back to the campus. When Lucas asked him to clarify, the man didn't answer, as if Lucas had only thought the question, not uttered it. What had Andrew seen in him? A little patch of his brain wondered whether Andrew might have seen a vestige of his former attraction to other men, especially his teammates. But no, it couldn't be. That was not consistent with how he saw himself in the world now. Andrew could only mean that in being with Angie Lucas was looking for a professional gain, the letter of recommendation Angie kept pushing for. Was this hostile behavior related to Angie's emotional distance from him? But why did she also act so coolly to her mother?

Later, when they were both in the living room of their apartment, reading and preparing for school the next day, Lucas looked up at Angie. He considered telling her about the full exchange with her father in the pub, but there was an implied accusation in Andrew's allegation that he wanted to bury and not bring to light any more than he had to.

Chapter 9

Camp Marie

The summer of 1959 was brutal in Trenton. Heat-related deaths for the city's poor broke records. Window air conditioning units had become common by then, and most middle-class houses had them, at least in the bedrooms.

Andrew Miniaci turned thirteen that August, and only two friends showed up to his birthday party. The neighbors knew that the Miniaci home was not air-conditioned, and the party was at three in the afternoon. The two guests sweated through their starched shirts before they finished the puddles of melted ice cream, and were gone before four o'clock. Andrew's sandy hair was plastered on his skull, and his sweat-soaked shirt clung to his bony frame. Dora, his mother, had brought them bowls of ice cubes from the kitchen so they could cool their faces.

Dora had tried to have air conditioning installed in the house, at least in the bedrooms, but Chester, Andrew's father, had refused. It was a waste of money, he said. Home air conditioning was a relatively new development, just ten years old, and humans had slept well without it for millennia before that.

The day of the party, Chester stayed in his office upstairs, one of three bedrooms in the house. He was an accountant and did much of his work there, sometimes sleeping there on a twin bed. He kept the office locked, and allowed Dora to clean it only once a month, under his supervision.

Andrew shared a bedroom with his brother Max, who was fifteen, two years older. They had asked to have a fan in their room for the nights when the heat did not abate, but Chester had refused that, too. Boys don't need fans, he said.

The Saturday after Andrew's birthday, Dora was in the garage sorting through accumulated junk. The heat had not let up. Chester had declined Dora's request for help. He was preparing for a conference in Philadelphia, which he went to four times a year.

"I'm going to need help, Ches," Dora said the night before. "The tables and chairs are too heavy for me to move alone." She was a tall woman, near six feet, and had strong arms from her college days in field hockey. She hardly ever asked for help.

"Let the boys help you. I need to get ready for this conference," he said before locking himself up in the office for the night. He was short and overweight, his waist an equatorial line between narrow shoulders and tiny feet that could only take little steps.

Dora asked both boys to help her after lunch, but Max had plans to go to the community pool with friends, and Andrew said, "It's too hot, Mom. Let's do it another day," and sat down in front of the TV.

When Max got back from swimming, he asked, "Where's Mom?" Andrew was still in the living room watching TV. "It's four o'clock. She's usually cooking in the kitchen by now."

Andrew had not seen her since lunch time. "She must be in the garage, sorting stuff for the garage sale."

Max went to the garage, and Andrew heard him yelling.

Dora was on the floor, a floor lamp tumbled beside her, the shade crushed. There was blood on the lampshade and on her forehead.

By the time the ambulance arrived Dora was conscious and sitting up on the floor, her back against boxes of junk. Andrew had brought her a glass of ice water and paper towels for the forehead gash. Max had gone to their father's office upstairs and knocked and yelled for him outside the locked door, but had gotten no response. "I'm not even sure he's in there," Max said when he got back to the garage.

Dora refused to go to the hospital. It was the heat in the garage, she said, and the EMT's agreed. The temperature in the garage was 107; the thermometer in the kitchen read 95. They bandaged the wound and left.

Dora sat in the kitchen for a few minutes with her glass of ice tea, then started preparing meatballs for dinner. Andrew rinsed the spinach as she instructed before putting it in the steamer. The heat in the kitchen made him dizzy, and he feared his mother might suffer another collapse.

Chester came out of the office just before dinner time, looking rested, untouched by the turmoil that had transpired. When they had sat down, Andrew told him what had happened an hour earlier. Max was busy serving himself first, before anybody else.

"You shouldn't have been doing that in this heat," Chester said when he heard about her collapse.

Andrew and Max had talked before dinner. Why hadn't their father responded to Max's call for help? Andrew felt that today had been the epitome of his aloofness. But Max had simply shrugged when Andrew had expressed anger.

Andrew looked at Chester helping himself to Dora's meatballs and spinach, making a big pile. Today he despised the obscene mound on his father's plate more than usual, although he had seen him heap enormous portions for years. "That was just foolish," Chester said as he brought the towering plate closer, "doing all that heavy work in the summer."

Dora said nothing. She looked at her own plate of food, as if Chester hadn't spoken. Max appeared oblivious to the exchange, but Andrew sat seething, cutting his meatballs with his fork, ignoring the knife, which he knew his father did not like. "Your knife is there for a reason," he had often said. Andrew scooped a forkful of spinach into his mouth and chewed with his mouth open, making a show of the revolting green bolus as he looked at Chester, who was too busy eating to notice.

There was a difference in Dora after her collapse. She was less energetic, less ambitious about fixing elaborate meals or doing projects. Things she usually took care of — sweeping out the cellar, washing window screens — went undone, Chester's minimalist presence of no use.

She was only forty-two, but she started to leave her hair untinted, and grey streaks ruined her oak and honey mane, a former source of pride.

Dora's change in vitality frightened Andrew. He realized for the first time the potential for frailty in his physically powerful mother, as if peering into a glass ball in which he could see an infirm old woman, needing, not dispensing, help. His complacency about his future — he had been a lackluster student — was replaced by a need for becoming a support for Dora, and for being a source of pride, never concern. He distinguished himself through high school. When it was time to apply for college, a guidance counselor called him down to his office and told him that he had been selected to receive a full scholarship to Princeton.

Max was already two years at Rutgers when Dora drove Andrew to start his freshman year.

One morning during their summer break in late July, after Andrew's first year at Princeton, the two brothers were in the kitchen, fixing breakfast. It had been a difficult night for them: humid, the puny, ancient fan they had moved from the living room useless, and neither had gotten much sleep. Andrew had been surprised at his mother's appearance when he first got home from school two weeks before. She had looked haggard, dark blue circles under her eyes deeper than they had been the past few years.

"Mom," Andrew said now when she walked into the kitchen. "Something wrong?"

"No, just tired. I was clammy all night, up a lot." Andrew looked at Max, who was busy mixing his cereal and did not appear to register the exchange, nor their mother's pale, sickly appearance. She had already showered and dressed, and he could still smell the jasmine soap from her shower. Andrew could not stop looking at her. "Stop staring. I have an appointment with my cardiologist this morning for a check-up." She had been diagnosed with an arrhythmia a few months ago and was on medication.

After she left, Chester came downstairs from his office, where he had spent the night, to get a second cup of coffee.

"Dad, I'm worried about Mom," Andrew said. "She's not sleeping well. She says the heat keeps her up at night, and she's looking terrible."

Chester filled his cup. "It's summer," he said. "It'll be cool again in a few weeks."

"Let us buy her an air conditioner she can put in the bedroom window. They're really efficient now, they don't cost much to run."

Chester was shaking his head before Andrew had finished speaking. "Absolutely not," he said. "Then the two of you will want one too, then one for the living room, then the dining room, then the kitchen." He took a sip of his coffee as he turned to leave. "Slippery slope. All that electricity. Money down the drain."

Andrew looked at his brother for support in persevering, but Max just shrugged.

A few days later, Andrew woke up at seven, the sheets and pillowcase on his bed soaked from the humid overnight. His underwear was still damp, sticking to his bony hips. He went downstairs to the kitchen and saw Dora sitting at the kitchen table. Even in the dim light coming in through the window over the sink he could tell she was pale, her lips a greyish lavender.

"Mom. What's wrong?" he said as he went to her, ignoring the fact that he was almost naked.

"I haven't slept half the night," she said. She was panting, taking deep breaths every other word. "My left shoulder is killing me, and I can't catch my breath." Her hair hung in limp, wet strands.

Andrew sat down opposite her and watched her breathe, her eyes bulging in fear. He got up without a word, went to the wall phone, and dialed the operator.

This time the EMT staff asked few questions once they saw her. They put an oxygen mask on and put her on a stretcher. "She's probably having a heart attack," one of them said before they had even done an EKG.

She spent a week in the cardiac unit, recovering from the infarct. When she was being readied for discharge, the social worker saw Andrew and Max at the bedside, and told them the cardiologist wanted to meet with their father. "You'd better call him and tell him yourself," Andrew said to the social worker that day. "Coming from you, he might agree to come to the hospital." Chester had gone to see her twice that week.

Dr. Sakov showed up right on time to Dora's room on the appointed day, when Chester had promised to be present. The physician was Chester's age, more or less, late forties, stethoscope draped around his neck. The thick lenses of his glasses made the brown eyes seem too small for his angular face. He sat down on Dora's bed and took her hand in both of his. He addressed his comments to her, occasionally glancing at Chester.

"The damage to your heart is significant, and permanent. You won't be able to do what you're used to doing. You'll need help around the house."

Chester sat with his arms crossed.

"No extremes in temperature. I know this occurred in the middle of a hot night, and the social worker says you were sleeping without air conditioning."

Dora nodded.

"From now on, in hot weather, you have to stay indoors in an air-conditioned room."

Andrew and Max looked at Chester, whose face showed concern now, lips parted, eyebrows up.

"How about fans and ice packs?" Chester asked.

Dr. Sakov shook his head. "If that's all you have, it's be better than nothing," he said, "but heat and humidity can put a severe strain on the heart muscle."

On their way home from the hospital, Chester drove, and he stopped at a hardware store. Andrew and Max stayed outside, looking at patio furniture on sale. They wanted to replace the heavy wooden stuff with something lighter for Dora to handle.

Chester appeared, carrying a large fan in its cardboard box.

"What's that for?" Max asked.

"Your mother. She can sleep with it blowing right on her. It's very powerful and very expensive."

"Dad," Andrew said, then stopped, caught himself before he said something he would regret. He had felt a blinding anger in the hospital when he heard that the heat had contributed to the heart attack, and had decided then that he would take things into his own hands before he and Max left for college. They would buy and install a window air conditioning unit in the bedroom where Dora slept, nowadays mostly alone, and there would be no discussion.

Max objected when Andrew told him about his plan later. "He's just not going to let that happen. You know he'll have it taken out as soon as we're back in school."

"Maybe not. We have to at least try. This is our mother's health, Max, in case you haven't noticed. Are you always going to go by what Dad says or wants?"

They decided to talk to Dora about it, and she agreed with Max. "There's no point. He'll have it taken out and you'll have wasted your money," she said, and Max nodded. She appeared even weaker than she had in the hospital. Andrew relented, but he feared she would not live long enough to see him graduate in two years. He and Max found a cleaning lady who came three times a week, and Chester begrudgingly agreed to pay her salary.

At the end of summer, when it was time for them to return to school, Dora was still debilitated. She took the stairs up to the bedroom slowly, stopping half way to catch her breath. Andrew would cringe and break out in nervous perspiration when he saw her do this. He felt as if she were slowly slipping away from the living. When he left for Princeton, he hugged her long and tight and swiped his eyes before he pulled away.

A few months later, one evening in early December, Andrew got a call in his dorm from Max, whose voice was shaking. "Dad's been in a car accident. It must be bad. They want us to go to the hospital right away."

"How's Mom?"

"She sounded okay on the phone. She asked me to call you. Can you meet us there?"

Neither Max nor Andrew had a car yet. "I'll get a bus to Trenton tonight, and I'll take a cab to the hospital."

When he got there, he was met in the emergency room waiting area by Max. "He's gone," he said, and hugged Andrew, who hugged back for an instant before breaking away to go find his mother.

In mid-December, two weeks after the funeral, Andrew was home for winter break from Princeton before Max. It gave him a chance to spend time with Dora alone and get a feel for how she was handling the loneliness, although she had only been alone ten days while Andrew and Max finished their terms.

"I still expect him to come down the stairs, and I think I hear him several times a day. It's strange being the only one here." They were in the kitchen, where she was making lunch. He saw that she did not seem distraught as she spoke. She looked puzzled, but not grieving.

Andrew was relieved his mother was making an complicated tuna salad, with lemon zest and chopped dill. She had not made any elaborate dishes since the hospitalization in the summer. He remembered her always wondering aloud whether their father would join them for dinner. If any of them knocked on his office door, all they got was a growled "I'm busy." And yet, if they started a meal without him, Chester came into the kitchen with anger draped over his pudgy face.

Dora mixed good Dijon mustard into the tuna salad. Chester had never allowed it in the house. "French's is good enough," he had always said. Yesterday in the supermarket Andrew had put it in the shopping cart without her noticing, and he had seen a disturbed look on her face when she saw the jar at the cashier's. But now she was doling it out liberally and folding it into the mayonnaise.

"Can you boys help me go through his things?" Dora asked them when Max got home two days later. She had recovered much of her strength, thanks to new cardiac medications, and was not shying away from physical work. She still got short of breath if she overdid it, but the cold days in December gave her a boost. "I've been through his clothes in the bedroom closet, but I haven't tackled his office yet."

"I've never even been in there," Andrew said. He finished the last of the mortadella and provolone sandwich, and wiped the mustard off his chin.

"Me either," muttered Max, not taking his eyes off the magazine he was looking at while he ate. "I'm not really interested in going into that office."

"Well," Andrew said, "it's a chore, not an amusement. I don't really want to go in there either."

Max kept his eyes on the magazine. "It'll be easier for you. You didn't seem all that upset when he died."

Andrew got up and put his plate in the sink, then sat down again, reached across, and closed the magazine Max was looking at.

"What the hell do you think you're doing?"

"You're still part of this family, even if your daddy has gone to heaven."

Max's eyes bulged. "Just because you had no feelings for him. Not like I did." He got up and took his plate to the sink.

Dora said, "Boys. Please." Her mouth was stretched in a slash, as if she might cry, and she covered her face with her napkin.

"He was a decent father to you maybe, for a few years. But by the time I came along he couldn't give a shit." Andrew's voice was restrained, matter-of-fact.

"He was our father. Whatever's going with you I don't know, and I don't care." Max left the kitchen, and they heard the car that had been Chester's being driven out of the garage.

After lunch, Dora gave Andrew the key to Chester's office. She had found it in his wallet, which the hospital had given her after he died.

The door to the office opened without a sound — the lock was well-oiled. Although there was bright sunshine outdoors, there was scant light coming in through the heavy yellow drapes covering the window, and he turned the light switch on. Table lamps flooded the blue walls with light. The trim and the door of the closet were painted yellow to match the drapes.

The metal desk was neat, two stacks of paper, a telephone, a blotter. A full-length mirror hung on the door of the closet. Andrew noted the narrow, well-made bed along one wall, with a fresh set of folded sheets on top of the blue chenille bed-spread.

He became aware then of the heavy, musty air. The office was warmer than the rest of the house on this sunny, December afternoon, and he went to the window hidden by the drapes to open it an inch or so. When he parted the curtains, he was surprised by the heavily scuffed paint of the window frame and sash, in sharp contrast to the pristine painted surfaces of the rest of the room.

A square object on the floor was covered with a white sheet, accounting books stacked on top. He would start the cleanup by putting these tomes in plastic bags. When he lifted the books, the sheet slid off the square object, and he pulled it off completely.

He jumped backwards as if he had uncovered a python, fell over the desk chair, and onto the floor. An air conditioner. He scrambled up, eyes fixed on the window unit. The shock he had not felt when he saw Chester's mutilated body in the emergency room descended on him now. At the time, he had been aware of the absence of grief, but had focused only on comforting Dora, holding her tight, hoping his embrace would be enough to protect her heart.

He went downstairs, closing the door to the office in case Dora came upstairs. He didn't want her to discover the secret without some preparation.

She was in the kitchen, washing up the bowl she had used to make chicken parmigiana. He was comforted by the smell of garlic and onions he had chopped for her.

"Is Max back?"

"Not yet," she said on her way to the refrigerator, but when she glanced at him she stopped. "What's wrong? You look like you've seen a ghost."

"Mom, why didn't Dad want an air conditioner in the house?"

"He said it was expensive to run. You know that."

Andrew didn't want to tell her, didn't want to be the conduit for evidence of his father's duplicity, but he didn't see any other way. "Mom, Dad had an air conditioner in his office."

Dora gave a stifled chuckle. "Don't be silly, Andrew. How could he?" She looked at Andrew's face and sat down at the table across from him. "Andrew? What are you talking about?"

The even-tempered crack in her skepticism without evidence of agitation relieved him. "Come. I'll show you."

Dora swayed unsteadily when she saw the air conditioner, and Andrew reached out for her. The health of her heart was foremost in his mind, and he made her sit down on the desk chair. She looked at him, shook her head. "I can't believe what I'm seeing. How can this be?" She looked off into space, then at Andrew. "Did you know about this?"

"Of course not. I just found it, not ten minutes ago."

Dora looked around the room, and at the things neatly arranged on top of the desk. She started opening the desk drawers one after the other.

"What are you looking for?" Andrew asked.

"I don't even know. Who knows what else I might find. It's like I've lived with a stranger for twenty-six years."

The bottom drawer was locked, and she went back to the top drawer, took out a key she had seen and unlocked it. She took out what looked like a diary and a long chrome key and put them on top of the desk.

"Not even a photograph of his family on the desk." She shook her head slowly a few seconds, as if trying to understand. "Bastard. He let his family swelter in the summer while he slept in comfort."

Andrew went to the closet and turned the knob, but it was locked.

"Here," Dora said, holding up the long chrome key she had found in the desk. "Try this. Let's see what other surprise awaits us in there."

There was a light cord in the closet, and when Andrew pulled it and the bare bulb went on he saw clothes hanging on a rod, tightly packed. There were brightly colored blouses, skirts, and dresses, with paisley and flowery patterns. "Mom, are these yours?"

Dora got up and stood at the closet door. "What is this?"

"Aren't these yours?"

Dora fingered the silk blouses, the fine wool skirts. "No," she murmured. She held the sleeve of a silk turquoise ball gown, rubbed it between her fingers. "No. I've never seen these before." She looked at Andrew as if she awakening from a dream, blinking. She looked down at the women's shoes lined up neatly on the floor: pumps, high heels, Mary Janes. "No. These aren't mine. This son of a bitch also had a mistress?"

A cardboard box sat on the floor under the skirts. Andrew dragged it out of the closet to the middle of the office and opened it. Inside they found dozens of photographs of women holding drinks, dancing, or posing with their arms around each other. But no. They weren't women, and in most of them he could see his father's unmistakable round face, wearing a dress, a wig, and lipstick. In one, a full-body image, he was standing alone, wearing a blue pillbox hat, a polka dot dress, and clutching a black purse. Next to him a wooden sign as tall as he read "Camp Marie."

"A stranger," Dora said, holding the photograph. "I've been a fool." She sat back down at the desk. "What did I ever do to deserve the life I've had with this man? My whole life has been a mistake."

The arrow went through Andrew. He went to her, feeling like a little boy trying not to cry, and he put his arms around her shoulders. He was surprised at how much comfort he wanted from embracing her.

"Not you," she said, wiping his face with her hands. Her own eyes were dry. She got a tissue from her pocket and dabbed his eyes. "Not my boys. You're all I ever had. The rest of it has been crap."

It took a few days for Andrew to stop being short of breath every time he thought of going back into the office to clear it out. Max was incredulous at first when Andrew told him, and he took him up to the office and left him there alone. He did not want to be a support for Max as he confronted their father's deception.

After a few days, as winter break was winding down, Dora showed her rare temper when she found out the office was still not cleared out. "You are not leaving me with that mess up there," she yelled at them one afternoon as she made chicken Tetrazzini. Andrew looked at Max, and together they went upstairs and started. "Don't forget the air conditioner," she yelled at their backs.

"Do you want us to put it in your bedroom?" Andrew asked.

"Put it out on the sidewalk. I'll buy a new one," she said.

After the room was empty, Andrew went back to it alone. It was still filled with treachery. The selfishness, the aloofness, the despotism, all became entangled with the crossdressing, and he would forever distrust men who did not conform to the traditional masculine role. He turned the lights out, locked the door, and put the key in his pocket. Just to be sure, he tried turning the white porcelain doorknob, which did not budge. He hoped Dora would agree with his plan to leave the room as it was for a few months, or years, or maybe for the rest of their stay in that house, as if a horrible death had taken place there.

Chapter 10

Arendt and the Law

Lucas kept philosophy as his major, and read voraciously, well beyond the required texts. He was obsessed with society's perception of what was good and what was evil, acceptable and not acceptable behavior. He read Arendt, Fromm, Nietzsche.

He was particularly intrigued by the theories of Hannah Arendt. At first he thought they were vague, abstract. But in her writings, he found resonance with his experiences and his perceptions of how society treated those who were different. Arendt postulated that evil and wrongdoing were nothing more than a failure to understand the effect of one's actions on others when they resulted in harm. And these actions deserved punishment.

He thought about the punishment he had received from Coach Gomez. Had Lucas been insensitive to how his holding on to his teammates would affect those boys? Had his getting so close resulted in harm to them? He didn't see how. He thought Arendt's theories solid, a template for justice and honorable behavior, and he didn't see how getting physically close to the other boys had damaged them, even if they didn't like what he was doing. They could have just told him not to play that way. He did not think he had received just treatment from Coach Gomez, and could not understand how his own father, a lawyer, had failed to see that.

He adjusted to life with Angie, her need for his time. When he wasn't focusing on schoolwork, he wanted to read, go to the gym, run laps on the track, but she wanted to watch movies with him, go to museums. She taught three yoga classes a week at a local studio, and she walked the two miles, instead of riding the bus, so that it would take up more of her free time and Lucas would have the time he needed to go to the school gym and workout. Her kindness and considerateness touched him, kept his affection for her kindled, and he relented and watched the old black and white movies made before their parents had been born.

The gym held an interest that he did not articulate to himself, but which he felt deeply and movingly. In the showers, he looked furtively at the men, and if he got aroused he hid the evidence behind a towel. His looking at the naked men was irresistible and exciting, and with no thought to act on what he was desiring, he gave it no label. Mysteriously, it did not seem to exist once he was dressed and on the way home. Still, even without a label, the images of the well-built men in the shower intruded when he was making love to Angie. He could still be aroused by her, but less intensely, and he responded to her touch and caresses once they were in bed and lights were out. But once they were in the middle of love-making, after penetration, he visualized whatever man he had last seen in the gym that week.

"I'm just no comfortable around your dad, Ange," he said whenever she proposed visiting them, which she did now only when she needed extra cash, or when they visited the Hudson Valley and wanted to take them out to dinner. Either way, Angie seemed to be in a hurry to cut short their visits.

"He's just a grouch. He's been rough with me too. And he'll come in handy as a reference for you for law school."

The few times they got together with her parents, he avoided speaking to the man, or even looking at him much, and Angie's father reciprocated and all but ignored him. But Angie was relentless in touting Lucas' academic accomplishments, his making the dean's list consistently. Lucas remained silent as her father nodded his head without looking at him, and her mother cooed, "Isn't that wonderful," with glazed eyes and often through a mouthful of food.

Two years later, with the strong letter of recommendation from Angie's father that she campaigned for, along with excellent grades that resulted in a summa cum laude diploma, he was accepted into every law school in New York that he applied to. He wanted to stay in New York, not just because it was close to his parents, but because now in 2006 the city was full of gay men who were more outwardly visible than they had been in years, now that the AIDS epidemic was in retreat. Without articulating it to himself in so many words, he feared if they moved to the hinterlands he would be too far removed from men whose presence reassured him. Staying in New York was the harness he wore as he jumped on the trampoline of his fears.

Angie graduated magna cum laude with a degree in business administration, and she was hired by a wealthy charitable foundation on the East Side of Manhattan. They found a tiny studio apartment not far from her job, and Lucas only had to cross town to get to law school. Both sets of parents supplemented their income in subtle but significant ways: Lucas' tuition came from his parents, and they used Angie's clothing and vacation allowance for basic living expenses.

"We should get married," Angie said to him one Sunday as they strolled in Central Park. It was May, almost a full year after their graduation from college, and the fragrant flowering trees and fields of daffodils infused Lucas with optimism.

"Sure."

He hadn't thought about it seriously, and had no timeline for it in mind. But here he was, living with her for four years, going to law school probably thanks to her father, despite their strained relationship after the third and final private conversation in the pub. Marriage would further his submersion in normalcy, a state he felt he was at the threshold of entering and wanted to reaffirm.

He had seen some breathtakingly beautiful men in New York. There seemed to be many more than he had seen at Vassar, including some in law school, and some at the gym where he worked out. One of them had approached him one afternoon, asking Lucas to spot for him while he did bench presses. "I'm Harry, by the way," the man had said, letting his hand linger in the handshake. He was shorter than Lucas, with brown hair over his ears and a beer belly that stretched the tank top, but his shoulders were swollen with muscle. "Come a little closer," Harry said, face up on the bench, grabbing Lucas by the hips and pulling him in. While he was spotting, Lucas let his hands drift from Harry's elbows down to the bushy armpits, and when he touched the hair his breath quickened, as if he couldn't get enough oxygen. Later in the shower Harry had turned and faced him, smiling, as he soaped his groin. Lucas saw the beginnings of an erection covered in suds as Harry continued to rub his hands over his genitals, and Lucas turned away when he saw his own erection starting to appear. He turned the water to cold and stood under it as long as he could before walking out of the shower to dry himself off, still in view of Harry. This arousal was on a deep, animal level, and he squelched it for the sake of being among the accepted majority, as he had during his football days in high school. Still, he considered looking at Harry again and waiting for him by the lockers. But once he was dressed he resolved not to pursue it. Giving in to that desire would be a selfish, thoughtless action that would hurt Angie if she were to find out — Arendt's very definition of wrongdoing. He had to leave those desires behind.

That night, when the lights were out, Angie turned to him and draped her thigh over his. When he didn't respond, she slid her hand under his tee shirt and caressed below the navel, just above the pubic hair, and let her hand amble down towards his penis. Lucas felt no arousal, but he touched her arms tenderly. As she continued to play with his genitals, he felt embarrassed and distressed at his lack of response. He tried to think of Harry, remembering the unmistakable arousal he had felt, but it didn't work. His penis shrank beneath his pubis, and he turned away with "I'm sorry." In the morning, when she straddled him and he lost his morning erection, she got up and went about the business of getting ready for work without the usual conversation.

Now in the park, walking next to Angie, he didn't see any reason not to get married — it was what people did. "Let's do it." He ignored the signals of the sexual fiascos, which were becoming more commonplace, and which Angie believed were due to stress from law school, as he had said.

"Only one thing, though. I don't want my parents at the wedding." She stopped and kissed him. "Let's just you and me do it in City Hall, downtown."

"Won't they be hurt, or upset with you?"

"Maybe. But I don't want them there. It's a long story."

"Fine."

They continued walking, although he wondered what had happened that she wanted to exclude her parents. He remembered how short she had kept their visits, always seeming in a rush to say good-bye to them. But he had never understood the need for a big to-do in order to marry someone anyway, and was fine with a small, private ceremony. He didn't see that there was anything to celebrate.

"We'll leave my parents out of it too, then, although they won't be happy about it. But will I hear your story at some point?"

She stopped and looked at two tall, blond boys in their late teens, dressed in white polo shirts and shorts, playing tennis in a near-by court. They were fluid on their long legs, and floated across the clay surface, as if held aloft and made to glide by invisible wires. Lucas was struck by their elegant grace. Angie turned to Lucas and buried her face in his shirt. She did not make a sound, but he could feel the cloth of his tee-shirt getting wet where her face was tucked, right by his armpit. When she pulled away he saw that her eyes were red, the lashes wet. "At some point you'll get the full story." She paused. "I had a brother once." She turned and kept walking on.

They married a month later, in June, and survived their parents' storm of disappointment at not been invited or informed ahead of time.

"You always wear the same cologne," Angie said to him one night in bed, a month after the marriage ceremony in City Hall. It was one of the many nights, the majority of them now, when they didn't have sex. He was finding it progressively more difficult to get aroused by Angie's touch. The novelty of another person's warmth and genital stimulation that had fueled his wanting to be with her back in college had receded almost completely, and he no longer felt any passion for her body. He continued to claim mental exhaustion from school, and tried to satisfy her sexual needs without an erection, usually without success. On those occasions, as would happen in later years, she would be silent and distant the next morning.

"The scent lingers so," she said that night, turning to him. He was on his back, facing the ceiling, and she put her hand on his belly, still hard and rippled from the years of football. He had managed to stay in shape by going to the gym where he had met Harry. She shifted her body so that her head was closer to his. "What's the name of it?"

"Halston."

"Where do you put it on? It smells like it's coming from your head."

"On my neck, around my ears," he said, turning to face her, but moving away, closer to the edge on his side of the bed, so that her hand fell on the sheets between them.

"Is that where men usually wear cologne? I thought guys put it on their shoulders and chest." Her voice was softening with drowsiness, and she took her hand back.

"I don't know. My father never wore cologne. I only saw my mother putting on perfume."

"How come it's the only fragrance you wear? Don't you get tired of it?"

"Oh, it reminds me of someone I knew once, someone I was very fond of." He closed his eyes. "One of my older cousins, who moved away from New York many years ago."

"What was his name?" Her voice was drifting into sleep.

It had not been a cousin. One of the guys in the high school football team had let him use his cologne after showering. He was thin and sinewy, the team's kicker, and they were the last two in the showers, toweling off in the locker room, not long after Coach Gomez's talk. Lucas, still chastised from the coach's lecture and the meeting with his parents, hesitated when the boy offered his cologne. He just wanted to get dressed, avoid eye contact and arousal. But the young man, a redhead with a mound of orange pubic hair that Lucas wanted to touch, splashed some on his palms and rubbed it on Lucas's shoulders, standing close to him. The man had then put his hands on Lucas's shoulders, spun him around, and put some more cologne on his back, massaging his muscles, and ending with a slap on the buttocks that ended as a caress. Lucas had covered his tumescence with the towel as best he could before turning around to face the smiling man, and he didn't want to speak his name now. Nothing had come of the episode and the mutual attraction. Lucas had made sure that they were never alone in the locker room again, and he had tried to forget him. He was suddenly wide awake now, and saw that Angie was already asleep. "Cole," he said.

Chapter 11

The Bonfire

Angela knew her brother Matthew had been there to greet her when she first came home from the hospital, when she was two days old. Olivia, her mother, had told her how Matthew, age three, had wanted to help change her diaper, had asked where her penis was, and how could the diaper be wet if she had nothing with which to pee. She knew these things as if she actually remembered them, her mother had told the story so many times.

Matthew had the long, sinewy body of a ballet dancer, a lankier version of their father. He had his mother's cheekbones and his father's blue eyes, and his gold hair lay in busy curls.

Even from her early teens, her friends dressed up and wore lipstick if they were coming to visit, just on the chance that he'd be home. "He's so hot," they would say when they caught a glimpse of him in his tennis uniform. His thick thighs, incongruous with the El Greco-like length of the rest of him, stretched the white fabric of his shorts.

"Are you doing anything this afternoon?" Angela asked him on Saturday. They were in the large kitchen, just finishing lunch at the oak table. The sun through the window over the sink bathed the counter and the African violets.

"Nothing much. Just hang out, maybe see some friends." He popped the last of the Cuban sandwich in his mouth, wiped the pickle juice running down his chin. He always used two napkins.

"Good," Angela said. "How would you like to drive me and my friend Dolores to the movies? They're playing *The English Patient* downtown."

"You two are still friends?"

"Yeah. Why not?"

"I heard you told her she was fat and should start wearing make-up." Matthew got up and went to the sink with his plate.

"I didn't say she was fat," she almost shouted. She whacked the top of the table with her napkin to clear the crumbs, which hit the wall. "All I said was she should go on a diet and wear some lipstick once in a while, look like something. Who told you?"

"Her brother."

"He's got a big mouth."

"Don't be an asshole to your friends, Angie. That's all I'm saying. But yeah, sure. I can drive you guys." He paused, cocked his head, and looked at nothing in space. "Yeah, that works. It's supposed to be a good movie. I'll have to see if I can borrow Mom's car."

"I already asked. She's not using it."

He shook his head, but he smiled, and Angela smirked back. "It's okay if Dolores and I sit by ourselves in the front of the theater? We just want to have fun. We won't get into trouble."

"Sure." He left the kitchen and went to make a phone call in the den.

Sixteen, with his new, limited driver's license, for daytime driving only, Matthew drove them in their mother's Volvo. The movie theater was not far, right in their small town of Maplewood, New Jersey. Angela and Dolores went off to the front row when they had gone in.

"Meet me on the sidewalk as soon as the movie's over," he said to them before they disappeared down the aisle. "Don't make me wait."

During the show, Angela went to the restroom. Near the last row, off to the side in an empty section of the theater, she saw Matthew sitting next to another man. When she had just passed them, and was out of their line of vision, she looked at their faces, illuminated by the light from the screen, and saw that Matthew was sitting next to George, a thin, effeminate boy she recognized from Matthew's class, handsome, with a fine, long nose and a mane of black hair. People in school talked about him. He was shy, despite his good looks, and seemed to have few friends, unlike Matthew.

In the car later, after they had driven Dolores home, Angela wondered why Matthew had not mentioned that he was going to meet George at the movies. As they turned into their block, she said, "So you sat all alone during the movie?"

Matthew hesitated. "Yes. Of course."

"Oh," she said as they pulled into the driveway. She had heard him mention George, and knew they played tennis after school with the tennis team. Why wouldn't he admit to sitting next to George during the movie? The fleeting mystery was quickly replaced by an understanding that George's effeminacy and Matthew's furtiveness might be related.

She had seen them playing tennis after school, along with other boys. Although Matthew called other friends on the phone, particularly the guys in the school band, she had never heard Matthew speaking to George. And he spoke to girls only when they called him at home, which was at least once a week.

"It's for you again," her mother Olivia said to him, smiling, when a girl called on Sunday afternoon. Matthew took the call from the extension in the den, in privacy.

"I think it's the same girl from last week," Angie heard her mother whisper to Andrew, their father. He was older than Olivia by ten years, already balding, and had an imposing build and posture. "Third week in a row," her mother said, giggling.

"Why does she keep calling you?" Andrew said to Matthew later, after he hung up. "Don't you ever take the first step?" Angela could imagine that challenging tone of voice with his students at the law school. The call had come at the end of lunch, the day after they had seen *The English Patient*. They were clearing the table.

"I do," Matthew said, picking up glasses and silverware. "But she calls anyway."

"Why don't you go out with her, already?" Olivia shouted from the kitchen through the open pass-through.

"You haven't gone out with her?" Andrew asked, borderline annoyance in his voice.

"Third degree," Angela sing-sang, smiling at Matthew, who grinned back with long, even teeth.

"Young lady," Andrew said. He stood up to help Matthew clear the glasses.

"Angela, butt the hell out," her mother yelled from the kitchen. "He doesn't go out with anybody, Andrew, in case you haven't noticed. Only with his buddies in the band."

"Or to play tennis with George," Angela chimed in, smirking, as she finished her ice cream.

"Angela, shut up," Matthew said as he took her dessert plate.

"Why don't you take some of these girls out, Mat?" his father asked as he came out of the kitchen. "A movie on a Sunday afternoon, then ice cream or pizza afterwards." He put his arm around Matthew's shoulders and led him out of the dining room to the den.

Afterwards, Angela and Matthew sat at the kitchen table doing homework while their mother watched TV in the living room. Their father was doing paperwork in the dining room, adjoining the kitchen.

"I know why you haven't gone out with that girl who keeps calling," Angela whispered, even though the door to the dining room was closed. Matthew looked up from his workbook with a slight frown. Angela continued: "I was looking for my tennis racket this morning, the one you borrowed to practice with George when his broke. I couldn't find it in the garage, so I looked in your closet, way deep in the corner."

Matthew's eyes opened wide. "So?"

Angela smiled. "I won't say anything. Don't worry. It's okay." She got up and went to the door leading to the dining room, held her ear to it, then got down on the floor to peer under the door to make sure their father wasn't standing nearby. "Those magazines are cool. Such hot guys, doing sexy things." She gave him a sly smile.

Matthew blanched. "Angie," he said in a hoarse whisper, glancing towards the door. "Angie, please don't say anything else." He paused, swallowed dry, and looked again at the door to the dining room. "I'm keeping them for a friend. They're not mine."

"Come on, Mat," she whispered, starting to giggle. "It all makes sense now. I don't care if you're gay." She got up again and leaned across to kiss his cheek. Matthew pulled away, closed the workbook and looked down at the cover, not making eye contact. She sat down again. "Do you have a boyfriend?"

Matthew's mouth dropped open as he glared at her.

She was smiling. "I'd like to meet him. Is it George? I think he's cute."

"Angela, stop it." He gathered his things and left the kitchen.

He waited until they were alone in the house two days later, then said, "FYI, the magazines are gone. I gave them back to my friend."

She did not tell him that she had seen a large garbage bag in their outdoor trash bin, a type of black bag that their parents rarely used, and that when she had looked in, she had seen the magazines. Or that she had waited until dark that evening, with the excuse of wanting to look at the stars for science homework, and had moved the bag to a neighbor's garage bin down the street, in case her parents noticed the unusual bag and looked in it.

A few days later, on Saturday, he asked his mother in the kitchen if he could borrow her car the next day, Sunday afternoon. She was standing at the counter with Angela, teaching her how to make pasta. "Can I ask what for?" his mother asked. She was an older version of Angela, dark hair and eyes, petite frame. The Sicilian genes had skipped Matthew and showed up in his sister.

Matthew spoke in a voice that was too loud, and glanced at Angela. "I'm going out with that girl who's been calling here. Fran."

Angela's mouth and eyes opened wide for an instant, and when her mouth closed the jaw was jutting and the lips were clenched thin. She walked out of the kitchen without a word, and didn't look at him.

"Angie," Olivia called out. "Where the hell are you going? I thought you wanted to learn this."

Sunday evening Matthew got home from his date at seven, just as dinner was starting. He joined them at the table in the dining room.

"How did it go?" Andrew asked.

"All right," Matthew said.

"All right?" Olivia said. "Just all right? You don't sound very excited. You're going to see her again, or what?"

Matthew looked at Angela, who normally would have made him laugh by rolling her eyes at their mother's exuberance, but she was making a point of looking straight ahead at the sideboard across the table and not at him.

"Maybe," he said. "We got something to eat, so I'm not hungry. I'll go read in my room." He looked again at Angela, who kept her eyes on the sideboard.

Over the next few weeks, Matthew dated three times, always a different girl. Angela remained cool, and did not sit in the dining room with him again after dinner, preferring to do her homework now in her own room. Doing homework together in the dining room had been an excuse for them to spend time together, no conversation expected. Angela always cherished the silent, physical closeness. One evening, two weeks later, there was a knock on the door of her bedroom while she was doing homework. "Come in," she called out.

The door opened slowly, and Matthew's head appeared. "Can I come in?"

Angela was propped up on her bed with a book. "Sure," she said, and turned her gaze back to reading. Matthew sat at the foot of the bed.

"Angie, why are you so angry?"

"Because I'm disappointed. You disappoint me."

"Why?"

"Because you're taking the chicken's way out." She raised her voice. "You've never been anything but up front with me, and with your friends." She closed her book. "When I was being cruel to Dolores, you called me on it. And when Jeremy, that guy who plays trumpet in the band, called George a faggot, you told him off. I heard about it from Dolores." Her face was starting to redden and distort. "You're always up-front about stuff." She pummeled the bed with her fists. "Going out with girls is not who you are, and you know it."

Matthew looked down at his lap, took a deep breath, and then looked up at her. "Okay, Angie, you win." He paused, as if unsure whether to go on. "You're right. I'm gay, and George is my boyfriend." There was a ghost of a smile on his face.

Angela's stormy expression softened into one of smug satisfaction. "I knew it."

"But I can't let Mom and Dad know. How do you think they'd react?"

"Mat, this is 1997. Being gay is not such a big deal any more. Even men with AIDS are living normal lives. How can you be ashamed of who you are?"

"I'm not ashamed of being gay, Ange. But I don't see what choice I have. You've heard how Dad talks about gays. Faggot, this, homo that. And Mom, with her going to mass and the priests blaming gay men for AIDS? Please." He shook his head.

"So what are you going to do? Hide who you are from them?"

"I guess. For now, anyway. It'll be easier when I go to college."

"I think it's going to be very hard for you. But I'll keep your secret, Mr. Butch man."

Matthew laughed. "Don't make fun of me when Dad takes me target shooting next week. He wants me to go hunting with him in November."

"Hunting? You? Mat, you don't even like to swat flies."

"It's okay. I think it'll be nice being out in the woods early in the morning."

When Matthew turned seventeen just a few weeks later that September, Andrew and Olivia bought him a brand new Honda sedan, cobalt blue and already gleaming in the driveway when he got out of bed that morning. Angie joined Matthew on the driveway, and they hooted in celebration and sat in the front seats before they got ready for school.

"I'll teach you to drive next year, when you turn fifteen," he said to her that afternoon as they sat in the Honda after school. She hugged him and kissed him on both cheeks.

"You want to go to the homecoming game next week, Ange?" Matthew asked in early November. It was the first time he'd be driving to the big annual event.

"Of course," she said. "Can I bring Dolores?"

"Sure."

At the stadium, she stood close to him during the bonfire, the initiating ritual of every homecoming game. The huge, violent flames always frightened her. Afterwards, she sat with Dolores to watch the game while Matthew sat with the marching band. He was the only person not in the band who was allowed to sit in the special, elevated bleachers, and she watched him with pride.

Later in November, when hunting season started, she prayed that he would be unsuccessful in killing a deer. She had watched without commenting as Matthew went to target practice with their dad, who also taught him how to clean the two rifles in the gun case in the den. She knew that shooting a deer would haunt him with remorse, and she was relieved when hunting season ended without a killing.

Deep into the winter, on a cold Sunday afternoon in February, the phone rang. Matthew had not gone out on dates with girls since November, and the girls had stopped calling. This time, Andrew picked up in the den, where he was reading some legal opinions. Angela was in the living room with Dolores and another friend, watching a disc of *My Fair Lady* on their new TV set. Her father came into the living room, looking angry. "Do you know where Mat is?" he asked her with a growl.

"He's in the dining room, I think. He's doing volunteer work for the ASPCA."

Andrew stomped to the dining room, and without entering brayed, "It's some guy on the phone for you, Mat. He said his name is George, and he sounds queer."

"I'll take it upstairs," she heard Matthew say, then saw him taking the stairs two at a time.

She didn't see her brother the rest of the afternoon, and at dinner time Olivia said, "Where's Mat? Dinner is ready." Olivia went upstairs to his bedroom, and a few minutes later she was back.

"Where is he?" Andrew asked, annoyance in his voice.

"In his room. Doesn't want to come down, says he's not hungry. He doesn't look so hot, but he says he's okay."

Andrew looked angry again. His eyes were swelling and his cheeks were red. "He got a call from a guy named George this afternoon," he said. "I thought it was a woman at first, but I think he's just a fag."

Angela put her forkful of salad down and looked down at her plate. "Dad," she said, shaking her head.

"Don't chide me, young lady," he barked.

"Andy, what's wrong?" Olivia said.

"You should have heard what this guy sounded like, Olivia."

Angela got up from the table. "Angie," her mother said. But Angela was out of the room and climbing the stairs before anything else could be said.

She knocked on his door, and when he didn't answer she inched it open, afraid of disturbing him. He was lying in bed face up, forearms covering his face. "Mat?" she said.

He didn't move at first, said nothing, as if he hadn't heard her. She sat on his bed, put her hand on his chest, and he started sobbing.

"Mat, Dad's being a jerk. Please don't be like this. He'll get over it."

He sat up, shook his head. "No," he said through the muffle of fluids, "he's not going to get over it."

It was then she noticed the bruises on his forearms.

"What happened to your arms? Looks like you got beaten up."

Matthew hesitated and looked away.

"Were you in a fight?" She couldn't imagine her brother in an altercation.

"It was Dad. He came upstairs and grabbed me and shook me after I spoke to George on the phone. He told me not to have faggots calling here again."

"Oh, my God," she said, and she reached to touch the bruises, wanting to make them disappear, but Matthew pulled his arms away.

A seed of hatred for her father settled deep inside just then and began to germinate, mixed with a devastating despair, nothing she had ever felt before. Her vision blurred a few seconds, and she felt her heart pounding.

He got up and went to his chest of drawers, and from the top drawer took a keychain. "Here," he said, "take this key, keep it safe. It's a duplicate of one I have."

It was a small brass key, an inch long. "What's it for?" she asked.

"You'll know when the time comes," he said. "Keep it hidden and safe." He lay down again. "Please let me sleep now. I'm so tired."

"Are you going to be OK?"

He nodded, head on his pillow, eyes closed.

By Wednesday, news had reached Olivia at the beauty salon, where she was getting her hair touched up: the first AIDS case in the neighborhood, as far as anybody knew, had just been diagnosed.

"And you know who it is?" Olivia said to Angela and Andrew as they set the table for dinner. Matthew was in his room, where he had spent most of his time since the call on Sunday. "That boy George. The one who called here. My hairdresser says his parents are sending him to live in New York with his aunt. They don't want him here. Can you believe it?" she said, carrying the steaming meatloaf. "AIDS, right here. Where's your brother, Angie?"

"He said he's not hungry. He's going to stay in his room."

"What the heck did that pervert want with him on the phone, I wonder," Olivia said as she sat down. "Oh, well. He'll be gone soon."

Angela looked at her father, who was now silent, fists on either side of his empty plate, mouth tight. Her heart pounded. She had never feared him before. "I'm going upstairs to see if he wants anything," she said. "I'll be right back."

"Don't be long," Olivia called after her. "Dinner will get cold."

She heard the gunshot as she reached the second floor and almost fell back on the stairs behind her. She knew it had come from his room.

The first thing she saw when she opened the door, which in that instant held no significance, was the red splatter on the blue drapes. Then she looked down.

He was on the floor, face up, a circle of red widening on the blue carpet underneath his golden hair, still gleaming. His eyes were partly closed, his mouth open, about to speak. And then nothing: her vision went blank before she fell, unconscious. When she came to, surrounded by the emergency personnel, she saw Matthew's body a few feet away, covered by a black tarp. His blood was on the sleeve of the sweatshirt she was wearing. She was psychotic with terror, not believing what she had seen, and could only scream. Her mind registered nothing else until the burial.

At the graveside, she stood between her parents, her mother weeping soundlessly, her father moaning. He tried to put his arm around Angela's shoulder, but she hissed at him and moved away, next to Dolores. When the casket was lowered into the ground, her sobbing was so intense she could barely breathe, and had to lean on Dolores not to collapse on the sod.

There was a note her parents found on Matthew's chest of drawers that Angela didn't read until a month later, in March, when Olivia gave it to her in the kitchen and stood close by, watching her face.

> *Be careful with the blood. I may have the AIDS virus.*
> *This is the only way for me.*
> *The diary underneath this note is for Angie,*
> *for her eyes only.*

Olivia gave her the diary without looking at her.

The tome was bound in blue leather, with a two-inch privacy strap that went from the back cover to the front and inserted into a brass lock. The strap had been cut, its metal tip still secured in the lock. She looked at it, not understanding at first, then looked at Olivia, who was grimacing, grieving anew. Angela walked out of the kitchen without a word and went to her room. She put the diary deep in her underwear drawer, next to the hidden brass key, where it remained untouched until November.

That summer, after the school semester was over, Angela had not recovered. She still felt disconnected from the world, not knowing when she was hungry, unsure about her ability to go up and down stairs. After dinner, she read and wept in her bedroom. She did not join her parents in the living room for TV as she had done when Matthew was alive.

One evening in July she ventured downstairs. She was dizzy, as she often was these days, and took the steps of the stairs one at a time, as if she were an old injured woman. She went out to the backyard. The fireflies were doing their dance, something she and Matthew had watched together just last year. It had been five months since his death. She reached her hand out, wanting to hold his, and the absence shattered her again. Without him life did not seem possible.

Olivia knocked on her door just before bedtime.

"Honey, I have something for you," her mother said when she entered. Angela wiped her eyes with tissues she kept at the bedside nowadays.

Olivia was carrying a sheaf of notebook paper an inch thick, held together with a rubber band. She held it out to Angie, then stepped away from the bed again.

Angela said nothing. She saw that they were poems in Matthew's longhand.

"We found these in his closet when we were cleaning it out," Olivia said, voice unsteady. "I thought you should have them."

"Did you read them?"

Oliva gave the ghost of a nod. "Some, but I didn't really understand them. And your father didn't even look at them. He wants them burned, but I thought if he wrote them, you probably want them."

"Why does he want them burned? You said he didn't look at them."

Olivia hesitated. "He's afraid he's going to read something he won't want to see. You know." She paused, then whispered, "Something immoral, like about his sickness."

Angie didn't understand. Did her father think Matthew had AIDS? "What sickness, Mom?"

"You know, his homosexuality," Olivia said just above a whisper, pausing between "homo" and the rest of the word.

Angela's face flushed. "You're calling his being gay a sickness?"

Olivia nodded. "It's what the Church says, honey. When he took his own life it was God's punishment."

Angie dropped her head down, chin on chest, dark curls flopping. She took the sheaf of Mat's poems, covered her face with them. "Get out of my room please."

She read the poems several times. Through them she felt Matthew's spirit, could hear his voice. She considered reading his diary now, give herself more of him, but she did not want to partake of the words her parents had violated. She would not share what was to have been exclusively hers.

The last poem in the collection was her favorite, perhaps because it was unlikely to have been read by Olivia, or perhaps because the ink he had used for this poem alone was green, the color of hope.

costAric An

I have dreams of my peaceful alien in

the shushing breeze, hammock swaying.

In wakeful moments

storms of worries, menacing threats.

Alarms and sirens wail,

loud so. Rules that devour

life, little lucks, little goods.

And then digging:

burrs that spin and drill the heart,

ogres that crawl in and tear,

unravel our souls and torture

the day, until we sleep again.

Send them away — let the lullaby lilt

efface these specters of doom,

xenophobes, while my peaceful alien and I slumber.

She read it four or five times over several days before she remembered that he liked acrostics, and when she read it again, his cleverness brought a smile that slid into a fit of weeping. She did not understand how the planet could still spin into days and nights without him.

When homecoming weekend came around in early November, nine months after Matthew's death, she hadn't gotten her learner's permit yet, although she was old enough now. She didn't want either of her parents teaching her how to drive. She had always thought her brother would be the one to do it.

She went to the homecoming game with Dolores, whose mother drove them. The diary, still unopened by her, was in the knapsack she was carrying. She wanted to preserve the schism that the violation had caused, and let the regret of never having read the diary be a perpetual reminder of her parents' treachery.

The usually-frightening bonfire was, as always, before the game. This time the heat mellowed the chill of the November evening, and in Mat's blue sweatshirt she stood without fear next to Dolores in the crowd that encircled the enormous flames. A towering black man, muscular, was standing a few feet from her. He seemed to be with two other men, both white, and he was chiseled-handsome, wearing a Yankees base-ball cap, a bomber jacket, and tight blue jeans. She stepped over to him and took the diary out of the knapsack. "Excuse me," she said. "Would you throw this into the fire? I don't think I have the arm for it."

"Sure," he said, smiling, teeth catching the flames, and despite the sissy throw he pitched it right into the center of the blaze. She saw a distinctly different flame flare up where the diary landed. A fresh plume of dense, grey smoke swirled elegantly before dissipating.

"Thank you," she said.

"No problem, girlfriend," the man said, still smiling.

Indeed, I wish you no problems, she wanted to say — long life to you. But she only smiled at him. She kept her eyes on him, hoping to engage him further, not wanting the exchange to end. Her brother might be alive and as happy as this man if he had had different parents, and she took a step towards him, but the man had already turned away to talk to his friends. He was on to other things now, and would soon disappear from view. She could only smile at the back of his head as he walked away.

The empty knapsack's lack of weight was unbearable. She walked to the bleachers with Dolores to find a seat near the band. She would not soil the sleeve of Mat's sweatshirt wiping the wetness from her cheeks and nose.

Chapter 12

Substrate

Lucas closed the biography of Hannah Arendt he was pretending to read. He was sitting in the narrow armchair he preferred, in a torn yellow tee-shirt and black shorts. Angela, on the leather sofa a few feet away, looked up from her laptop with the frown that was ruining her face every day now. Lucas forced a grin and went into the bedroom of their small New York apartment to pack for his week at the monastery. He wanted to do it alone, to start his break from her now, as soon as possible. But she followed him in, looking glum, getting the duffel bags out of the closet.

"How many long sleeve shirts should I pack?" She didn't look at him. Lucas wished she wouldn't be so annoyed that he was going to a religious retreat. He wished he could convey to her how much he loved her. He said it regularly, and had tried with embraces and kisses, but other signals he was sending, such as turning away from her in bed when the lights went out, spelled physical rejection, and eclipsed the affection he tried to convey. She was somber and shook her head as she went through his drawers, finding socks that were mismatched, something she had once joked about.

"I don't know," he said, not looking at her. "Brother William didn't say what the weather would be like." He lumbered around the bedroom, undecided as to what to pack. Lucas wished she would leave him alone. Through the open curtains of the two large windows he saw the evening sunlight shining amber on the building across the street. A pigeon flew to the window and perched on the sill. As he counted out the tattered briefs he would need for the week, and Angie folded shirts, he heard the bird's cooing through the glass, calling for its mate. He had a vision of opening the window and slapping the annoying bird off the sill. The threadbare underwear he was folding irritated him, suddenly. Why didn't he do as Angie did, throw out worn clothes, buy new ones? He looked at the heap of embarrassing rags on the bed, pretending to be self-absorbed and unaware of her presence, although in fact he knew exactly where in the room she was, what she was doing every second. The resentment held in her posture and her silence were like a shrill siren.

"Why don't you leave me alone?" he almost said.

Lucas had contacted the monastery of Saint Augustine a month ago. He had chosen it because of its remoteness, partially. It sat on the east slope of a two thousand-foot mountain in the Adirondacks, not far from the Canadian border. He had researched religious communities online, seeking spiritual counseling so he could continue doing his job: prosecuting drug-related crimes. The work he was doing tormented his conscience, because he knew that drug addiction was a health issue that needed medical treatment, not incarceration.

The agnosticism he had grown up with was still with him, and he felt hypocritical looking at a religious community for enlightenment. But he had seen how Simon, a man he had met in law school and who had great artistic talent, had found answers at a religious retreat. Simon had been unsure about which path to follow, the practice of law or setting up a studio to work with his oils. He had gone to a therapist first, who after months of expensive weekly sessions had determined that Simon's need to succeed in law was due to his Chinese parents' expectations and his need to please them. "No shit," Simon had said. "I could have told him that the first session." He had then gone to a Buddhist retreat in search of answers, and had returned committed to stay in law school, but also pursue his artwork seriously.

Lucas' job as an assistant district attorney in New York had become nearly impossible to perform without a consuming guilt. One recent case, a month ago, had been the last straw. A young black girl, an orphan after the 9/11 attacks ten years ago, had been tricked into prostitution while scavenging for food on the street. She had subsequently become addicted to drugs and developed AIDS. Lucas had been instrumental in putting her behind bars at the age of twenty-three, although what she really needed, he had known even as he pursued her sentencing, was treatment for addiction, and rehabilitation.

His doubts about the morality of what he was doing started soon after he got the job. And right after that, his sexual indifference to Angie worsened. His sexual appetite for her had receded during law school, but now it was non-existent. He saw it as cause and effect, and was convinced that if he could be at peace with his work, his sexual interest in Angie would return. He refused to connect his attractions as a teenager, which seemed to disappear almost completely after he met Angie, to his lack of sexual interest in her. His attraction to men had not disappeared completely, he recognized. There had been those moments after college, in law school, when he had been aroused by men. But overall, he believed, she had jolted him into heterosexuality.

And yet, even now there were those lingering looks at men in the subway, those sustained exchange of glances with handsome guys on the street. He attributed that sexual thirst to his inability to be aroused and sexually satisfied by Angie, and for that he blamed the mental exhaustion that came with the work he was doing.

The furtive thoughts he still had were the reason he did not want to see a therapist about his job — he didn't trust them to focus on his job, thought a therapist would go off in those very tangents he didn't want to explore. All he wanted was to still his conscience about his job, and he wanted to do it efficiently in the week that he had off. If Simon had done it, so could he.

"Tell me why you want to spend time with us," Brother William had asked on the phone when Lucas called the monastery.

"I'm having problems at work, and I think it's affecting my marriage."

"What kind of work do you do?"

Lucas explained, then, "But I'm not sure the work I'm doing is ethical."

"Hmm." Brother William paused. "I don't see an obvious connection. But let's set up a week in August. There will be plenty of work in the garden, and with our goats. We'll keep you busy, which helps clear the mind."

Lucas was relieved when Brother William agreed to his visit, already feeling welcomed, and had smiled at the phone as he hung up. The monk's voice had a soothing quality, and Lucas stroked the handset in its cradle, as if petting a cat.

"All he said," he told Angie now in their bedroom, "is that they do farming and that they have a herd of goats. He didn't mention anything about what clothes to bring."

"Well, good luck with the goats. They're smelly animals." Angela's voice was louder as she rammed his torn, folded underwear into the duffel bag. "Are you the same guy who told me last month he didn't want a cat around because of allergies?"

He was annoyed at this flare-up, brought his hand up to his brow and shielded his eyes from her. He did not want to justify his decision to spend time away from her any more. As he dashed to the bathroom to get toiletries, he placed a fleeting and what he hoped would be a mollifying kiss on her cheek. For weeks he had not allowed the opportunity for their lips to connect, and was far from wanting that show of affection now. All he wanted was peace, and to be left alone. She remained stony after the kiss, didn't look at him, and he felt another stab of exasperation. She took some of his torn underwear, wiped some wetness away from her eyes and nose with it, and threw it in the wastebasket.

That night they were silent as they prepped dinner together in the kitchen. Lucas seasoned chicken thighs with salt and pepper, then stuffed tarragon leaves under the skins. Angie poured them each a glass of white wine, their nightly routine while they made dinner. Conversation always became more relaxed and animated with wine, no matter the tensions of the day, but tonight they were silent as Angie cut the potatoes that Lucas scattered around the chicken in the pan.

Angie flung the knife in the sink suddenly, and turned to Lucas. "Are you having an affair? Is that why we're not having sex?"

Up to now, she had only hinted at having such a suspicion. "I guess you must be having fun elsewhere," she had said half-jokingly when his erections failed.

Lucas shook the roasting pan violently, and he closed his eyes. He stopped himself from raising his voice. "There's no one else." He turned to face her, dropped the metal pan on the counter with a clatter. "I've already told you I think it's my job. And I need to give this some thought."

"You haven't let me near you for three months," she said, grabbing the roasting pan with the chicken from him and shoving it in the oven. "And give what some thought? Us?"

He closed his eyes for a second, and took a deep breath before opening them again. "No, Angie, not us. You know I love you."

"Then show it." She moved to the sink to wash the knife.

"I hate this job." He had said this a dozen times, but his voice still rose in pitch. "I'm up at three every morning thinking about work. The guilt never leaves me." And then, something he had never articulated, but had thought about: "Sometimes I wish I could just end it all and be at peace." He was immediately sorry he had blurted it out, and the alarm on her face let him know that she understood what he meant. Angie looked down, put her hands on the edge of the table and leaned on it.

How absurd that he was wishing for death again without having any obvious struggles. They were both healthy, had enough income, lived well. The animosity between them had been sustained now for almost a year. He had thought about divorce these past few weeks, but no. He loved her, didn't want to push her out of his life. She had made him immensely happy once, the happiest he had ever been. The memory made his eyes glaze for a minute. When he focused again, he saw her chin down on her chest, eyes closed. She had remained like that since the moment he had obliquely referred to suicide. A sob almost erupted out of him, and he suppressed it with a dry swallow. The thought of suicide had entered his mind before, but he understood it to be an exaggerated response to a problem he was sure could be solved. All he wanted was harmony to return to their marriage.

"Do you think that other men who aren't happy at work just stop being physically affectionate with their wives?" She sounded earnest in wanting to know, not challenging.

Lucas covered his face with his hands. He didn't want to cry, didn't want to make the evening worse than it was, but her change from furious to conciliatory, almost to the point of being vulnerable, moved him. "I can't answer for other men," he managed to say into his palms. "This is just who I am."

Afterwards, the evening became gloomier no matter how much wine she poured. Like ink from an octopus, the sadness darkened the space around them.

They ate in silence in the small dining area, an extension of the living room. A year ago Angie would have said, "Yours is the best roast chicken, ever," but tonight she kept her eyes down on her plate and didn't finish, a rarity. There was a somber look to her face, different than the anger earlier in the evening, and again he regretted mentioning his death wish. Lucas kept glancing at her, trying to bridge the schism he felt he was causing, but she remained closed off, and his guilt about their unhappiness was like a centerpiece on the table.

"What are you looking for?" Angela asked him after dinner when they were in the kitchen cleaning up. Her tone remained changed, almost docile, not a trace of accusation. It was the same question Brother William had asked him on the telephone. When he said he was hoping that meditation might lead to inner peace about his job, Angela shook her head and said, "But a religious retreat, Lucas? You don't even believe in God. What's going on?" She opened the dishwasher and looked at him. "Really. What's going on?"

He closed his eyes before answering, partly from mental exhaustion, but he was also physically tired and wanted to close the door on her and on this repeating discussion. "I'm trying to understand myself more, what I want out of my professional life." He turned away and went on loading the dishwasher, not having the energy to rehash it all again now, eager for the getaway to the monastery in two days that would be a break from this tension.

She dropped her chin, curly chestnut hair flopping on her brow. She looked like a sorrowful child. He felt remorseful that he had made things worse by implying suicide, and he put his arms around her. His wide frame engulfed her small figure, and his ochre hair fell on her brown curls. It was the first embrace in many days, and a year ago it might have led to an erection and the bedroom. He kissed the top of her head, still scented of the pear shampoo that he loved to smell, and continued holding her without making another move. She freed herself from his arms and went to the living room, and he finished the cleaning up in the kitchen alone.

At bedtime, they each read, Angie a carnage by Stephen King, and Lucas *Our Lady of the Flowers*, by Jean Genet. Tonight it was Angie who without looking at him closed her book, turned out her bedside lamp, and murmured "Goodnight" as she turned away from him.

Lucas considered touching her shoulder now, he felt so much love for her, and such enormous guilt about being the cause of her unhappiness, about wishing for his own death. But he knew that even if she responded to his overture, he would probably not become aroused enough to engage in sex with her, at least not the sex he knew she expected. He had learned years ago that trying to please her sexually without penetration was futile and led to immediate resentment, and an angry distance the next morning. He withheld his show affection rather than risk another round of her feeling rejected.

He tried to remember the last time he had a good erection. It had been this morning, actually, as it was most mornings. In that first minute of wakefulness the images in his brain, leftover from his dreams, were often of his years in the football team, the horseplay with his teammates. But he knew he would lose the erection if he turned to Angie with the intention of nuzzling her.

He remembered their first years together in college, right after he gave up football, sexual and loving. The sex they had so frequently then had validated him as normal, a first for him. And after graduation they had enjoyed decorating this apartment they lived in now. They were the happiest years of his life, when he was finally inhabiting the skin he wanted, that of heterosexuality and mainstream acceptance. Law school for him, a good job for her, and New York's vibrancy to hold it all. Nightly they would pour wine and talk about the day, plans for vacation, who they'd see on the weekend. But while still in law school, his erections had started to fail. Desperate to satisfy her, he had tried to use the image of a naked Harry, the man who had come on to him in the gym so many times, and who never failed to get him aroused in the gym's showers. Other men he had met at the gym had also been overtly seductive. But he had never succumbed. And he managed to provide Angie enough affection and sexual gratification so that serious difficulties between them were kept at bay.

Things worsened significantly after he began this job, a plum position Angie's father facilitated for him through connections. It seemed at first like a great opportunity, but he wondered if that was part of the problem. The job was like a gift from a man who didn't like him. As he fell asleep, he fantasized about getting a transfer to another department in the District Attorney's Office, although he already had been told, several months ago, that it was not going to happen.

When he awoke, the thought of going to the office, in the Manhattan Criminal Courthouse all the way downtown, made him queasy. He had not slept well, the previous evening's combative atmosphere waking him repeatedly. He considered calling in sick, but it was Friday, and he'd be leaving for the monastery tomorrow. Taking an extra day off before a scheduled vacation was not a good idea. As he rode the subway downtown, he tried to imagine what Brother William looked like, what he was like, and whether he would be able to discern what was wrong and help him.

Brock Stone, the Assistant District Attorney he reported to, had been wanting to talk to him, but Lucas had been in court most of the week. He would find the time today. Brock was a heavy-set black man in his late forties, already a grandfather, and Lucas had always liked him for his no-nonsense but affable manner. The sleeves of Brock's dress shirts were perpetually rolled up, even when he put on his suit jacket to go to court.

Lucas unlocked the door to his office and walked into his cramped, windowless space, shelves full of law books, stacks of papers on the floor, and made his way to his desk. He left the door open to air out the mustiness. Within minutes Brock knocked on the open door. "Can I come in a second, Luke?"

Lucas closed his laptop. "Sure."

"You've been looking pretty miserable lately. Everything okay with you?"

"Well, so-so." Good. This was going to be the conversation he had wanted.

"Everything okay at home?" Brock paused and raised his eyebrows. "I have to wonder, because your productivity here has taken a dive the past three months."

Lucas wasn't expecting this. He moved his chair closer to Brock. "Actually, no. Things at home are not good. As a matter of fact, my work here seems to be affecting my home life."

"I don't understand. How's your work here impacting on your home life? You've let some cases drag on the past few months."

"Brock, everything I read about drug abuse and addiction, the crimes I'm supposed to prosecute, tells me it's a disease. These people should be getting medical help, not being put in jail."

Brock shook his head. "If it's a crime, we have a job to do."

"I can't help my conscience, Brock."

"You're telling me that because drug addicts and dealers are in need of medical treatment, they should get a break?"

"You should see the nitty-gritty of some of these cases. It's heart-breaking, sometimes."

"I've seen the nitty-gritty. For twenty-two years I've been looking at nitty-gritty. They break the law, we have an obligation to the social order, Luke."

Lucas put his forehead in his palms, and dug the heels of his hands into his eyes. He shook his head, wanting to be rid of the memory of the young black woman. He went to his desk and got out an affidavit the social worker on the case had filed, and gave it to Brock.

Department of Social Services
City of New York

June 22, 2011

Affidavit of Contact

Subject: Dorothy Spare

Interviewer: Jennifer Constanza, MSW

*Subject (Dorothy) being interviewed after arrest for drug posses-
sion and prostitution. Perceived by appointed defense attorney
and presiding judge to have possible mental/cognitive impairment
during initial hearing of the case.*

*Dorothy states she has no family or next of kin. Her grand-
mother...*

I be livin' with my grannie Lucretia since I be five, 'cos
my momma dead, and my father long gone. My momma dead
from drinkin' and usin'. My grannie cook breakfast at the twin
towers, you know. She always left 'fore I was up.

When the attacks happen I be in school, and Mr. Porter
from the principal office come to the classroom an' say, "Boys
'n girls, they been terrible accident at the World Center." So
ever'body askin' wha' happen, wha's goin' on, an' he say, "Two
planes crash into the towers, an' they be on fire."

I start screamin' 'cause of my grannie, but some of the
boys be hootin' an' hollerin' 'cause we goin' home, they be
so stupid. When I got home I turn on the TV an' I see bofe
towers down on the ground, and I pray my gran be able get out,
maybe she on her way home. I keep lookin' out the window at
the sidewalk downstairs to see if she coming.

I sat by the window until dark, prayin' hard to Jesus my
gran come home, but it was no use. That night I woke up

all the time, thinkin' I'm hearing the door open, like she be home, but I be dreaming. Next day I gone to all the neighbors, but nobody knew nothing. One a them say she goin' to call the police to come get me if my gran not comin', 'cause I be too young to live alone, and they goin' put me in a home for children.

After a few days I run out of food. I started goin' to the store an' takin' food when nobody lookin', put them under my shirt, but the cashiers those bitches saw me leavin' ever' day wifout nothin', an' next day a man from the store follow me roun' 'til I left.

I gone to MacDonald to git a job, but they say I be too young, only thirteen. They took the French fries sittin' on the shelf an' threw 'em out after a while, so I ax 'em if I could have 'em an' they say no, I have to pay for 'em. I went in back, where they keep the garbage, but a man come out and say he call the police. I gone back that night after they close but they be rats an' I was too afraid. So I gone back nex' mornin' before they open, an' got me some stale fries and buns.

A car stop by when I lookin' through the garbage. The man axes what I'm doin', and he say, look here, don't you have no mama and no papa? An' I say no, my grannie gone a week, I ain't got nobody else. I be afraid, but this man smilin', dressed real nice, an' he give me a small pipe, like Popeye smoke? an' he say if I suck on it, it make me happy. An' now I know it be crack, but then everythin' look good. So he say if I go wif'im he give me plenty a food.

I don't wanna talk about what Rudy, that be his name, did to me. But it was sex, you know. And he give me crack to smoke first. He didn't let me go outside. He brung other men in the house, an' I had to do them too, you know, an' they pay him.

Later, he send me out on the street to look for men after school hour' so nobody git suspicious. I thought I could git away, you know, go back to my grannie's apartment. I still had the keys. But I gone n' they change the locks, an' anyways I need the crack, so I had to go back.

Rudy always got me out of trouble somehow, after I see a judge in court. He tole 'em I be his niece an' ever'body else dead. I had no one else to live wif, so I never tole the truth about Rudy being no relation. An' I got AIDS now, too.

Dorothy is now twenty-three years old. She has had multiple arrests for prostitution and for having crack cocaine and other drugs on her person before this current arrest. She expresses herself in simple language, but she's intelligent. She wept several times during the interview.

By my signature below I affirm this is a vebatim account from the subject.

Jennifer Constanza, MSW

Brock seemed to only skim through it, and started shaking his head before he had even finished. "It's a sad story, for sure, but she's still a criminal. It's our job to prosecute these cases. Otherwise, what?" he said, getting up. "They keep using, killing themselves, dealing in it?" He started moving towards the door. "You just have to do your job, Luke. Leave society's problems out of it." He opened the door but stayed in the room. "We just do our job here. Consider this a warning." He left and closed the door.

Lucas went back to his desk, opened the laptop, but found he couldn't concentrate. He was preparing a brief for a court case in which a drug-dealer, a repeat offender who had stabbed a competitor, would be serving a long sentence. It was of the few cases in the past year he felt good about, and he needed to focus, but Brock's visit and his threat had shaken him.

He closed his laptop and went in search of Brock, whose secretary, Michelle, looked up from her typing when he approached her desk. "What's up, stranger?" She was around his age and divorced, with a wide pug nose that reminded him of a pig, despite her shiny brown hair and big breasts, cantaloupes in mesh bags. "I don't see you around any more."

"Is he in there?" He pointed to Brock's door.

"Nope. Said he had to step out for some fresh air." She looked at him with unblinking blue eyes. "You want me to let you know when he gets back?"

"Please." He started to walk back to his office.

"Hey, counselor," Michelle said to his back, and he turned around. "You're looking kind of stressed out lately. If you ever want to talk about work or anything," she said, smiling. "You know, blow off steam." She gave a little shrug. "We can go out for a drink or something."

"Thanks," Lucas said, and turned away. "Let me know when he gets back."

Twenty minutes later Michelle buzzed his line. "Hey, Brock's back. He's ready for you."

Brock was at his desk, and Lucas sat down opposite him in the only extra chair in the room.

"Look, Brock, I really have been trying here, but I can't do this forever."

"Forever? You've been here only a year." Lucas noticed that he did not move his chair to be closer to him, standard collegial behavior usually. "Hardly forever. You know how long I was in my first position in this office, going after delinquent traffic violators? Six years. Six long years of shitty work."

"It's a moral issue with me. I know you've already said no, but if there was another department I could transfer to I'd be okay," he said. He leaned forward in his chair, wiping his sweaty upper lip. "I mean, it doesn't seem fair that I'm seeking punishment for these poor jerks, while other guys are working on the aftermath of 9/11, prosecuting terrorists."

Brock leaned back in his chair. "They're bored and frustrated too." He was frowning now.

"You can't be serious. The two jobs don't have the same importance."

"Luke, the job of a janitor in a school is not as prestigious as the principal, but he's there to keep the whole thing going. Without him the principal wouldn't have a decent place to take a leak. Just do your job," Brock stood up. "I've told you before, there are no other positions available at this time." He paused and looked hard at Lucas. "Or you can leave."

Lucas felt his forehead sweating. "I'm going on a retreat next week, hoping to figure things out. If I'm able to find an answer, I'll stay on. If not, I'll start looking for another job."

Brock was nodding and his lips were in a tight line. He opened the door. "You're a smart, talented lawyer. But maybe this job is just the wrong fit."

Lucas walked back to his office, depressed that Brock was essentially threatening him with termination. Again his thoughts took refuge in what he had heard when he spoke to Brother William. Not just the content, but the way it had been delivered. The monk had exuded tranquility with his voice, and Lucas looked forward to his getaway.

Chapter 13

The Haloed Moon

The call from his mother came on a Sunday in November, just before mass.

"I have bad news, *mijito*," his mother Giselda said. "Your brother is very sick."

"What's wrong with him?" William asked. He cradled the phone on his shoulder while he tied his dress shoes. He heard his mother sobbing, the scuffle of a phone being passed, and then his father's voice.

"Can you come see your brother?" His father Alonso had a heavy Spanish accent.

"Papi, I can't just run to Miami. I'm working on my dissertation, and I have classes to teach." Shoes on, he stood up. His girlfriend Rosario was standing by the front door of their cramped apartment, ready to go, pointing to her wristwatch.

"Your brother Oscar is dying," his father said. "I can't say no more. You better find the time."

"When was the last time you saw him?" Rosario asked as they hurried to the church, four blocks away.

"Last Christmas. He seemed okay then." He kept his eyes down on the sidewalk, could tell she was looking at him.

"He still lives with your parents, right?" Rosario had never met Oscar.

"Yes."

Oscar had never had a girlfriend, and William dreaded what this illness might mean. He had read with relief about how the AIDS epidemic was now, in 2000, starting to trend down, although still claiming thousands of lives. "He's never moved out," he said.

"I guess that's good if he's that sick." She held on to his arm, and he could see her breasts bouncing in the cotton blouse. Those globes were what had attracted him initially.

William flew to Miami alone over the Thanksgiving weekend. Alonso and Giselda met him at the airport. He was stunned at how haggard they looked. His formerly plump father was thin, clothes flapping around him, and his mother's copper pageboy had grey roots. He had never seen her out of the house without rouge on her chalky cheeks.

In the back seat, William broke the silence as they pulled out of the airport parking lot. "What's going on with Oscar?" He leaned forward and spoke in English, easier for him, although his parents usually spoke to him in Spanish.

His mother turned around. "Oscar has AIDS."

He whimpered and fell back on his seat, his tongue stuck to the roof of his mouth. Oscar was younger by two years, twenty-five, and had kept his social life hidden. At the Christmas party given by a famous Cuban singer last December, which Oscar had taken him to, William noticed that he had greeted both men and women with kisses.

"But there's good treatment now," William said. "People are living longer."

"He waited too long, *chico*," Alonso said from behind the wheel, negotiating Little Havana traffic. "He was afraid to tell nobody. Not even his doctor knew, *coño*."

"I hope God forgives him," Giselda said.

"For what?" asked William.

"For being homosexual." Her voice was quaking. "He doesn't want to confess his sins."

"Talk to him," Alonso said. "Make him repent to God for being a *maricón*." He spat out the last word, and Giselda covered her ears, shook her head. William slouched in his seat.

In Oscar's small, stuffy bedroom in the modest, stucco ranch house, he did not see what had been his brother. Sitting up in bed was a skeleton covered in yellow skin, eye sockets black, lips drawn back in a macabre smile showing too many teeth. There were purple splotches of Kaposi's sarcoma the size of quarters scattered on his neck and chest.

He stood at the bedside, paralyzed, ignoring Oscar's open arms and forward incline, requesting a hug. When Oscar, losing his smile, gave up and patted the bed beside him, William sat, and forced himself not to recoil when Oscar took his hand. William's mouth opened in awe at his brother's appearance up close, and Oscar nodded and let go of his hand. Neither spoke for several minutes, and when they did, it was mundane: about the flight, the heat, and the fact that there would be no Thanksgiving dinner this year.

The horror didn't leave him: not on the flight back, not at home or at work. Oscar died in August of 2001, age twenty-six. William could not go to the funeral, resentful of his parents, not wanting to taint his grief with anger that on the phone they were more ashamed than sorrowful. And he found that his mourning was tinged with anger at Rosario's bigotry. "I feel sorry for your parents," she'd said when his mother called to say that Oscar had died. "It must be terrible to have a homosexual son and watch God punish him for it."

He hid his revulsion at her callousness, but it began to obliterate his affection and desire for her. In his studies in sociopsychology, he had been blasé and cerebral about the phenomenon of blaming the victim. First hand, it was hateful.

In September, a few weeks after Oscar's death, Rosario came home from work and her first words were, "We have to talk."

William looked up from his reading at the kitchen table. "What do you want?"

"You sound annoyed. I'm sorry, but it's important." The almond eyes were swollen in her caramel face.

"The defense of my dissertation is due next week." He closed the book. "That's important too." He turned his rickety chair to face her on the sofa, a few feet away.

"I'm pregnant."

"How's that possible?" They had been so careful about the timing. "Did you get your cycle wrong?" His tone was higher now, infused with accusation.

Rosario leaned back into the sofa, hands on her lap. "I kept close track, William. I kept you aware of my cycle."

He leaned forward and put his head in his hands. "Even if I get my degree in a few weeks, my job at the university is not enough if you have to stop working."

"The doctor said I'm two months along." Her voice trembled. "We have seven months."

"We won't have enough." It was a near-shout, and she flinched. "I'm sorry." He got up and went to sit next to her. He took her hand because he thought he should, although he didn't feel it. The sexual attraction was ebbing ever further, and there wasn't enough there otherwise. He had remained with her out of sheer inertia. Now it was too late to break up without the stain of abandonment.

"We'll be okay." He didn't really see how that could be true.

Rosario nodded. "We'll go see Father Flanagan on Saturday about getting married."

Nausea — a cold wave bathed his forehead and his nape. "Yes," he mumbled.

He awoke at two in the morning, tormented. Why hadn't he insisted on contraception? Rosario didn't want to go against church rules, and he had gone along, too eager for sex and for those breasts back then to challenge her and risk losing her. Abortion out of the question. But if the fetus was lost, somehow, an act of God. Or what if Rosario disappeared, went back to Puerto Rico or was taken by aliens or something? Poof. Gone.

The alarm went off at seven, and he heard her retching in the bathroom.

"I guess now we know why you've been sick in the mornings," he said, going into the shower. When he came out, Rosario was still in her pajamas on the bed. Normally she would have been dressed and closed up the sofa bed.

"Maybe I'll call in sick."

"I thought you didn't have any sick time yet." She had just started a job two weeks before as a secretary at a financial firm in the World Trade Center.

"I don't. They'll just dock my pay."

"Not something we can afford," he muttered. He finished getting dressed, went to her and forced himself to kiss her on the cheek. The reek of stomach fluids was still on her breath. "I'll see you tonight."

When he got to the university, it was just before nine. He always enjoyed his morning walk to work, and this Tuesday in September was a particularly beautiful one, with a clear cerulean sky, the air so dry the sun's fire was kaleidoscoped by the buildings' windows as if from shards.

He went to his office to prepare the lesson he'd be teaching, but could not concentrate. He felt trapped. If he never saw her again he would be untouched by her absence, relieved even.

His cellphone rang just after nine. Rosario.

He heard gasping. "There's been an explosion," she said between coughs. "There's a lot of smoke in the office."

"An explosion where?"

"Nobody knows. The building shook, and now there's all this smoke."

"Can you get out?"

"No. There's fire by the stairs. We're all trapped." She was gagging.

"Get down on the floor."

"I am. Everyone is — "

Dead. No sound. He called back. Nothing. Someone knocked on his door. With unsteady legs he opened it. Miriam, a colleague, with the news.

Two hours. He sees the images on TV in the staff lounge, where the faculty gathers: people flinging themselves out of windows near the top of the building, choosing death by impact over death by incineration. Then the collapse of one tower, and then the second. His calls to police stations and emergency rooms are fruitless.

Two days. He hears about husbands, wives, parents who go as close as they can to the site, as if to glean information, or maybe just to be near the loss. He reads about emergency rooms expecting a tsunami of casualties that remained idle, because there are no survivors. He had gone home at noon, made phone calls and watched TV for two days. Endless images of the towers' windows vomiting bodies and flames.

All his training in psychology is useless for his remorse, the guilt that he had wished Rosario and his future child would vanish. The body he had enjoyed so keenly at one point and had resulted in a new life, all of it incinerated, particles he sees in the air and wants to breathe in when he finally goes downtown. He wants to inhale the pollution of human ash not only as penance for his wish-come-true, but for surviving.

Two weeks, and the final revisions to his dissertation, delayed by the catastrophe, are accepted, the doctorate granted.

Two months. He gives away Rosario's things to the Salvation Army. It is only later he finds out they are homophobic and feels new remorse for having supported an oppressor of men like Oscar. He is awash with regret and shame. He can't seem to do anything right. At least he hadn't supported Reagan, whose administration ignored the AIDS epidemic.

He goes to see Father Flanagan, desperate for consolation. But face to face with the priest in the rectory office he is too ashamed of his death wish for Rosario to bring it up. Instead, he deflects, talks about his faith in humanity being destroyed by the savage acts. He says he needs to understand the human capacity for cruelty so he can do his work as a therapist. He doesn't say that he wants to forgive himself.

"There are no easy answers." Flanagan appears younger now and more low key than the cranky priest from Sunday mass, with his sermons about the imperfect goodness of humanity.

"What about this glory of humankind you talk about?" William is secretly asking not just about the terrorists, but about his own ruthless wishes. "How can I believe in that after this?"

Edmund Flanagan shakes his head. He takes off his black-framed glasses, spits on them and wipes them on the edge of his cassock. "All primates are capable of evil. You and me are not exempt. Haven't you ever had malicious thoughts you knew were cruel? Visions of harm befalling someone?"

He is a Jesuit, William knows, can argue for hours without taking a breath and always win. He leaves less than unconsoled: his remorse is refreshed. That night, sleepless, he looks out the window of his apartment. The moon is ugly, a sickly pale yolk with a fuzzy red halo, as if it is seeping blood.

Months go by. Professionally he thrives, but before and after work he is despondent. Only when he is in church listening to Edmund Flanagan does he feel consoled, that the aliquot of evil in humans is only that, and containable.

He meets with Flanagan weekly, and he gets a type of counseling he has no training in. They talk about human interactions, something he can understand, but with a spiritual dimension that is foreign to him and which ennobles the species, the priest says, sets it apart. The weight of his guilt lightens temporarily during their sessions.

"Tell me about joining an order, about entering the religious life," he says to the priest after a few weeks. He wants the cossetting he gets with Flanagan to be sustained.

The reverend, behind his desk, leans forward and clasps his hands. He is wearing a frayed grey shirt and stained jeans. "I've been expecting this. Go on a retreat first. With your education and your nagging intellect, you belong with my order." William nods. "I'll make some phone calls."

A few months later, after several retreats that brought him so-lace, he convinced himself that the monastic life would be the balm for the anguish he felt. He gave notice to the psychology department at the university, and entered a monastery in the Adirondack Mountains. As Brother William he vowed contem-plation, communal work, and chastity. He was twenty-eight.

As a member of the community of eighteen monks, he was expected to use his professional skills in the outside world. He worked at a nearby psychiatric facility, his salary going to the monastery, but he also had duties inside the walls of the enclave. He helped in the kitchen, the vegetable garden, and was assigned for a week in the infirmary.

"Prepare yourself, Brother William." Simon was a grey-haired monk in the monastery who worked as a nurse. They were about to enter the sickroom of a comatose brother on his deathbed. William had been assigned an overnight vigil. "He has lymphoma, end-stage, and it has spread to his skull, behind his left eye."

The monk was in bed, covered in a white sheet, only his head showing. His left eye was pushed out of its socket by what looked like a golf ball of raw meat, and the eye itself was resting on his cheek.

"It's hard to keep that eye covered," Brother Simon said, hurrying to the bed and replacing the moist washcloth that had fallen on the pillow. "Will you be all right when you're alone with him?" The monk's blue eyes, fringed with crows' feet, had a tired look.

"Yes," whispered William, still stunned by what he had seen. "It's only six hours," he muttered to himself. It was midnight.

"Just watch him and take his pulse if you need to. Don't do anything else. Come get me if you need any help, or if anything changes."

William settled into a wicker armchair near the single, narrow bed. The white cotton curtains were closed over the small open window, and a sink with a comb and toothbrush stood near the bed. He opened the book he had brought, Merton's *Book of Hours*. He could hear the monk's labored breathing in the silence, shallow, sibilant breaths, and saw that the chest, under the sheets, stopped periodically.

An hour later he looked up. The monk appeared to be resting, but under the covers the chest was no longer moving. William went to the bed and listened, tried to take his pulse as he had been taught by Brother Simon, and felt nothing when he put his index finger on the man's wrist, already cool. He went to find Simon.

"At last," the older monk said after he had confirmed the man's death and they were on their way back to their rooms. They had straightened the body and closed the gaping jaw. "I've been praying for this," he said as they neared William's room.

"For his death?"

"Yes. It was time."

"Because it was hopeless? He didn't seem to be suffering."

"No. Because the toll his illness has taken on the rest of our community has been huge. And the risks for those that had to clean his waste and bodily fluids," he said, shaking his head.

"Risks?"

"Yes. His lymphoma was AIDS-related." They were standing now in front of William's door. "He became infected years ago, well before he joined our community."

William's throat was parched and gritty suddenly, and his vision blurred. He opened his mouth, but could utter no sounds.

Brother Simon put his hand on William's shoulder. "We didn't see the need to divulge that, except to the brothers that had the potential for becoming infected."

William shook his head. "But I was assigned to his care. I wish you had told me."

Brother Simon's eyes hardened. "You were not exposed to bodily fluids, and he had a right to privacy while he was alive. Some might argue even now." The old monk turned his head and looked down the empty corridor. "We all have secrets we deserve to keep."

In his room, William undressed completely and washed his hands and armpits in the small sink. He turned the overhead lights out, forgetting to turn on the bedside lamp first. The room was dark except for the silver moonlight filtering through the white sheer curtains. He stood by the window and saw the August moon above the forest, three-quarters full, with a spectral red halo that announced coming rain, maybe a storm. The window was open, and the room was chilled by the night-time air of the mountain. He shivered and saw that his penis, that source of complicated pleasure for him, was shrunken and pathetic in the cold, a superfluous appendage now. He wanted to go to the toilet down the hall, but he stayed by the window and watched. A shadow, perhaps a deer, broke away from the tree-line of the forest, raced out of sight, and all was still again.

He looked at the moon again, pewter clouds dancing across it, propelled by the buffeting earthly winds. He wanted to scream at it, but went to bed instead under its watch.

Chapter 14

Retreat

The late summer foliage was lush from the window of the north-bound train from New York. The barren, granite slopes of the Adirondacks rose abruptly beyond the train tracks and seemed close enough to touch. The landscape was alien, forbidding, as if the Monastery of Saint Augustine were accessible only to the most determined. He ignored the book on is lap and stared out the window.

Angie was morose the morning of his departure, a continuation of the previous night, when she had ebbed from furious to withdrawn. She had gone to the gym right after breakfast, her Saturday routine, and said no more than "See you" to him as she left. Not even a kiss, as was usual when she left in the mornings. She had barely looked at him, despite the fact that he would be gone by the time she got back, and did not wait for him to finish saying how he was going to miss her before she closed the door behind her with a minor slam, gym bag over her shoulder.

On the train, Lucas read a biography of Saint Augustine. In the absence of any religious belief, he wanted to know at least the facts about the man for whom the monastery was named. In his duffel bags he carried a blank notebook. He would keep a diary of sorts, something to refer to in the future, just as he had kept class notes during his college and law school days.

He gathered his things when the conductor announced Hartwell's Crossing, the stop where Lucas would be met by Brother William. The train, with its cocooned, indifferent passengers, had been like an extension of New York, too close in atmosphere to the isolation and unrest at home. When he stepped off onto the platform, the silence and the fresh air lightened the weight of his bags and made his footsteps springy.

He stood under the tin roof. There were fields of corn on the other side of a two-lane road, and a mountain rose just beyond the farm. He was the only one that had gotten off the train.

A blue pickup truck was the only vehicle in the tiny parking area. As he walked towards it, he noticed a thin, bearded man dressed in a white shirt and brown pants leaning on the truck. The man began to walk towards him. "I'm Brother William," he said. He smiled as they shook hands. From their telephone conversation, during which the monk had sounded business-like, almost brusque, Lucas had expected an older, more imposing man, not this thin person close to his own age.

They began the climb up the mountain toward the monastery. Brother William chuckled as he blew the horn at geese crossing the road that he came close to running over.

"You said on the phone you wanted to spend time in introspection, something about your job."

Lucas looked out at the valleys below them. "I want to see if spending a week here can help me with some problems I'm having at work."

"Why here? Why not explore religion in your own community?"

Lucas didn't want to admit that he had no religious affinity, that he was looking for spiritual guidance for his conscience. "I'm hoping to concentrate on it here, in complete immersion, without distractions."

"I see. An escape from something?" Brother William smiled, and Lucas noticed that his teeth were startlingly white against his dark but graying beard. "What specifically made you want a retreat here with us?" He was still smiling, but when Lucas began to say something about work, Brother William cut him off. "That's what you said on the phone, but it's hardly ever about work."

They drove through a wrought iron gate in a stone wall that surrounded four brick buildings. Lucas could glimpse fruit orchards beyond the two-story structures that faced a central square landscaped with rhododendrons and roses.

Brother William led the way up the stairs in the dormitory building, then down a white corridor with several oak doors. Lucas detected a scent of incense and roses. His room was the last one on the right, and Brother William opened the unlocked door and stepped in.

"You see we're not in the habit of locking doors. If you want to lock yours the key is on the dresser."

He separated the white sheer curtains and lifted the window to air the room, which had white walls, and was just big enough for a narrow wooden bed, a small dresser, and a sink.

"Lights out by ten, and if you've brought a radio or music we ask that it be off by vespers at nine."

Lucas sat on the bed, suddenly tired by the trip and the heat, and with no desire to do anything else.

"Afternoon prayers in ten minutes in the chapel. Knock on my door, three doors down on your left, and we'll go together."

Lucas looked around the small, perfectly clean room, the cotton bedspread as white as the walls. He sat down on the bed, the cotton of the bedcover cool on his hands. The bed was beyond firm — hard. He lifted the thin mattress and saw that it rested on wooden planks. The austereness reassured him that the focus of his stay here would be spiritual. The view out of the small window was of a perfectly mowed lawn, with a tree line of evergreens fifty feet away. He wanted to remain in this quiet room, read, and rest. He unpacked the notebook that he meant to keep as a diary.

Day one. Saturday.

When Brother William opens his door, he is barefoot. The jeans he wore earlier are on the narrow bed, identical to mine. His feet are long and narrow, the second toe obscenely long, like it's someone else's.

We walk to the chapel, which is in a separate building, its main distinguishing feature the modest steeple. The pews are filling with monks dressed in brown robes, identical to the one Brother William wears. I'm still in blue jeans and yellow tee shirt, the only one not wearing a cassock. I try follow the service in the hymnal, chant along with the monks. It feels presumptive of me, like a child pretending to recite the incomprehensible words of a Shakespeare sonnet. A half hour later I wonder if I've made a mistake in coming to stay for a full week. I picture Angela at home, sipping a glass of wine, getting dinner ready. I

do not want to be there either, but I miss those eve-
nings when they had been fun.

I feel the impossibility now, not of meaningful-
ness necessarily, but of a center around which I can
form a content, if not happy, life. Here with these
strangers, I don't see how this week is going to help.
They could never care about me or my being at peace.

Brother William escorted him to the administrative building,
walking more briskly than he had this afternoon. "Brother Carl
manages the produce and goat cheese we make. He'll assign
you some work."

"Welcome, Lucas." Brother Carl smiled at him with
crooked teeth behind a bushy brown beard. He sat at a plain
oak desk in a cramped, small office. "Brother William wants
me to put you to work."

Brother William nodded. "It will help us break him
down." He grinned at Lucas.

"Let's see," Brother Carl said, running his grey eyes up and
down Lucas. "You're a sturdy-looking fellow. How about the
potato field? They're just starting to produce."

"Sure," said Lucas. He had no idea what to do with potato
plants. "Will somebody show me what to do?"

"Yep." Brother Carl stood up. "Brother James supervises
the crops. He'll go over it with you tomorrow before you start."

Brother William and Lucas walked back together to their
rooms. As they walked up the stairs in the dormitory, Lucas
was aware of the aura of silent reflection that was still surrounding them since the prayer service, despite the jokiness
with Brother Carl.

"I'm so unhappy at home," Lucas blurted out. "I hope I can find some answers here."

Brother William looked at him but said nothing until they were close to their rooms, as if the break in silence had been obtrusive. As they walked down the corridor, Brother William said, "Dinner will be over by seven thirty, and from then, until vespers at nine, will be for your private tutoring." They were stopped now in front of Lucas' room. "We'll have a discussion then, and you'll have time for your private reading."

Lucas unpacked the two duffel bags and lay down on his narrow bed, his head touching the simple oak headboard, of the same wood as the desk. It all seemed hand-made, even the doors to the hallway and the closet. There was no fan and no air conditioning, and the heat made him sleepy. He was awakened by Brother William knocking on his door to go to dinner. He had been dreaming of being in a vast, elegant room, with tables full of cakes and pies and no one else in sight.

The large, cheerful space that was the dining hall was filled with noisy monks who were dressed in brightly colored short-sleeve shirts and jeans. Dozens of conversations echoed off the white stucco walls and large windows with broad wood frames. They sat at a table for eight that filled up as trays of roast beef, mashed potatoes and spinach were brought by brothers from the kitchen. The monks talked about the heat and the lack of rain, the new litters of baby goats, local gossip.

"Did you hear about the cheese scandal at the convent?" Brother Kenneth was a wiry, clean-shaven monk, older than most of the others.

"Ah, the case of the non-organic mozzarella," Brother William said, and then turned to Lucas. "The nuns in our neighboring convent used supermarket milk to make their cheese when their own cows dried up but didn't have money to make new labels." There were chuckles and belly laughs.

"Did they get into trouble? Legally, I mean," Lucas said.

"That's right, you're a lawyer," William said. "No, they reimbursed their clients, and the state gave them a break. But I know they were worried about their reputation in the community."

Lucas stopped eating and put his fork down. "It's a good thing their good name wasn't ruined." He had his eyes on his plate. When he looked up, several of the monks were watching him, and on Brother Kenneth's face was concern.

The meal was simple but perfect, full of conversation and camaraderie. It was the most enjoyable dinner he had had in over a year.

The tutoring hour after dinner took place in the quiet library, a small room upstairs from the dining room. The walls were covered by shelves made of polished oak, from which Brother William selected literature for Lucas to read. The monk sat next to him at the small table, big enough for just two chairs. Lucas detected an odor of smoke and incense coming from the monk sitting close to him, the residue from the afternoon service. He leaned and tilted his head towards William, and felt unaccountably comforted.

"You mentioned a dilemma you were having at work when we spoke on the phone," Brother William said.

Lucas described his job seeking punishment for drug dealers and addicts. "But I know these people are addicted, and need to sell and take these drugs. It's a medical issue that needs treatment, not punishment."

Brother William remained silent, but nodded.

"It's been ruining my life at home," Lucas continued. "I lost my sexual interest in Angie when I started having doubts about my work. That's when the problems started."

The monk listened, looking at him with a calm gaze when Lucas spoke about his home life. It was the same look he had received at the dinner table from the other monks.

"I think we will be ready for a discussion of your marriage in a few days, after we have gotten down some basics about good and evil and punishment." Brother William paused, then fixed his eyes on Lucas. "And then we'll talk about your marital situation." He smiled and stood up. "From now on when you go to chapel you can wear the grey cassock in your closet."

"Ah. Should I have worn it this afternoon?"

"No. That first service you were an outsider, a visitor. But now I see you'll be part of our community for the week."

Lucas wondered later that evening what Brother William had meant by that. What had the monk seen since the service that had convinced him Lucas was sure to stay the whole week? Did other visitors leave before completing their retreat? He couldn't imagine not wanting to stay in this refuge.

The next day, after morning prayers at six in the chapel and a breakfast of eggs and hot cereal, Brother James, in charge of the potato crops, found Lucas in the dining room. Brother James was short and fleshy, with a pale round face and a flaming red beard, and together they walked to the field Lucas was expected to tend. The monk showed him how to pick potato beetles off the leaves and drop them in a container of alcohol. He piled up soil around each plant to prevent the potatoes growing near the surface from being exposed to sunlight, which would turn them green and bitter. The task was an enormous job to get done in one day, re-peated daily as new beetles, new weeds, and new potatoes emerged.

When the bells rang for noon prayer Lucas had made little progress, and the heat and the sun had worn him out. All he wanted was to take a nap. He hadn't had the need to take a daytime nap in several years.

After a half hour of communal prayer, and a half hour for lunch, he was back on the field, the heat now even stronger in the afternoon sun. He was relieved when he heard the bells for afternoon prayers. The day was beastly hot for August this far north, and the chapel steamed with the heat of the monks, who had put on their floor-length brown robes over their damp work clothes for the longest ceremony. Lucas' robe was the only grey one it in the chapel. The chanting that yesterday had seemed meaningless became hypnotic and emptied his mind of the day's work. He remembered instead Angela's rage the night before, and wondered whether she was still annoyed, but also found that the her tantrum's importance was receding. He wondered how he was acquiring this emotional distance so quickly, but the thought was interrupted by a sudden buzzing in his head, and he felt a strong sense of commonality with the chanting brothers.

Later in his room he undressed, dropping his sweat-drenched clothes in a heap. He wrapped a towel around his waist and walked to the shower room down the hall. He wanted to clean up before dinner and the session with Brother William.

There were three shower stalls for the six rooms on the floor, and he was all alone. In the small shaving mirror he saw some grey at his temples he hadn't noticed before. He hung his towel on a wooden peg, and let the hot spray run over him. The water flowing on the white-tiled floor was brown with dirt from his body and iridescent with his sweat. He saw it as evidence of his inclusion in this community's activities, and he smiled. But there was a deeper sub-current to the sight, of which he was only remotely aware, and that was the comingling of his very biology with the earth. He was reassured that

Brother William had been right when they spoke on the phone. The hard physical work would break down his defenses and make him see a clear path.

Back in his room he took off the towel and stood naked in front of the small mirror over the dresser. His body still showed the effects of his years of football, the muscled shoulders and rippled abdomen. They were fond reminders of the times he had connected physically and so euphorically with other men, as fraught with the risk for ostracism as those acts had been. He did not remember the last time he had even taken the time to inspect himself in a mirror and reminisce like this. The forbidden, usually repressed memories were a luxury to revive.

That evening after dinner Brother William met him in the library and handed him a short biography of Saint Augustine, as well as a copy of *Confessions*, a book the fifth-century church father and physician had written. It had laid the foundation for much of modern religious thinking, the monk said as he sat down next to Lucas.

"You chose well in coming here for your retreat if seeking punishment for drug dealers is making you uncomfortable," said Brother William, giving Lucas the two slender books bound in fine brown leather. "Augustine believed that love and compassion had to be part of every human interaction, that its absence was a failing that could give rise to sin. Or evil."

"Every interaction has to involve love and understanding?" Lucas frowned and fingered the pages of *Confessions*, as if looking for something. "Why is that relevant to me?"

"Because the drug criminals you prosecute are not taking into account the harm they can cause to others, especially their children, or to themselves. If they understood that and lived by it, they would not commit these crimes."

"I don't know how realistic that is today. It seems outdated. After all, Augustine lived in the fifth century."

"It's not outdated," Brother William said, shaking his head. "Have you heard of Hannah Arendt?"

"Yes, of course. I majored in philosophy, and in fact I've been reading her biography."

"Well, like Augustine, Hannah Arendt believed that compassion and understanding are essential to avoid evil and wrongdoing. She did her doctoral dissertation on Augustine, actually." Brother William got up from his chair, placed a hand on Lucas' shoulder, and walked to the bookshelf to look through the titles. "We have one of her books here. She proposed that evil is banal because it is simply action without compassion or empathy." The monk gave up his search and sat back down at the table, across from Lucas. "The drug dealers and addicts you prosecute, terrorists, Nazi war criminals," he said, enumerating on his fingers, "are all evil and punishable because they don't have any regard for the damage or death they cause."

"I'm not sure terrorists and drug users belong in the same category." Lucas remembered the young woman he had prosecuted for drug possession and prostitution. He sat back in his chair, away from the monk.

"It's a matter of degrees, but basically both are punishable."

"Brother William, I have colleagues that are still investigating terrorists connected to 9/11. I've seen the photographs. Body parts on the sidewalk, arms and legs, intestines scattered." Lucas shook his head, trying to get rid of the images. "It was pure evil. Where did that hate come from? It wasn't just thoughtless action."

"It was hatred, yes, and evil, but they saw us as always shoving our values down their throats. Also, they want a piece of the pie, and they think we have taken their share."

"You're not saying these terrorists had any justification?"

"It was an understandable political action without empathy for those they killed. So it was evil in the end."

Lucas saw that the monk's face was covered by the shadow of sorrow.

"You make it sound as if the misdeeds of dealing drugs and murdering thousands of people are in the same category." Lucas picked up the two books off the table, eager to leave. He could see the haunting eyes of the young woman he had put behind bars, whose life had been ruined by the collapse of the twin towers. And how many hundreds, thousands more were like her? He didn't want to talk to this man who was putting her in the same category as Osama Bin Laden.

"It's a matter of degrees, but yes."

"I was just a teenager when 9/11 happened," Lucas said as he stood up and stepped around the table, closer to the monk, "but I see a difference here. I think if you had been personally touched by the disaster, you'd think differently." He realized too late that he had been raising his voice.

Lucas saw that Brother William's faced flushed. "Whether I was affected or not is not really relevant," the monk said, closing his eyes for a few seconds. "We have to look at it through a wider lens."

Lucas watched as the monk pushed himself up to standing and took small, hesitant steps towards the stairs. He almost went to assist him as he would an unsteady, elderly person. The monk held on to the banister for a few seconds before he turned his head and said "Good night" over his shoulder without his usual smile.

Day three. Monday.

The sky is unnaturally bright this August evening. The storm that assembled this afternoon is past, and the air is light and dry. In the east, the sky is indigo. I don't dwell on the sunset. The rest of the community is in their quarters, and the common areas — the allés, the landscaped squares, the orchards — are sepulchral in their emptiness.

Brother William walks past me now with nary a glance, sometimes a nod. His smile, that luminous flash of teeth amidst the grey beard, does not appear. He withholds it as a husband or wife denies his spouse kindness in retribution for a wrong. His anger surrounds him like a poison haze.

When I'm not working or in chapel I try to read, but instead I walk the grounds looking for company. Everyone is busy with their own pursuits. The state of calm I was achieving here has been shattered. I am sensing the disorientation that the rest of my stay here would be without him. I know instinctively that solitude has benefits, but it is difficult. Why is it so hard to be happy alone? Why, whenever I am alone now, do I become thirsty for the company of these men, especially William?

I sit on a stone bench behind the dorm, where I have never seen anyone linger. I listen to the silence under the darkened sky, and it makes me feel faint.

Lucas' time alone in the chapel was not for prayer. He had not been moved in his agnosticism despite the religious environment. All the discussions he was having with Brother William were remarkably devoid of religious dogma, as if the monk had sensed that the element of faith was not part of Lucas. In the chapel he reflected on the day's labor and interactions with the other monks, and pondered his role in society as an administrator of punishment. He was beginning to be convinced that perhaps his role was not simply to be destructive of lives, but perhaps had a remedial, beneficial aspect to it. Evenings he strolled under the oaks and maples that dotted the spaces between the buildings and thought about these things, but also about his sexual feelings, which were becoming less repressed as he spent time away from Angie. Here, surrounded by these men, he observed their comfort with each other, their lack of guardedness about close physical contact that was not sexual, but affectionate nevertheless. They hugged, they put their arms around shoulders or waists, all without guile or awkwardness. Lucas envied these men, and vaguely considered his future if he were to stay permanently, if here his need for physical masculine contact might be satisfied without the need for sexuality and society's disapproval.

He ran into Brother Kenneth one evening, the wiry monk who joked frequently at the dinner table. Kenneth was one of the oldest in the community, in his late forties, with a smooth, shaved head and thick, ropy arms that were snug in the sleeves of the tee-shirts he wore. Lucas could pick out his loud, cascading laugh in the dining room, even when the monk sat far away, out of sight.

"Am I right that you're in charge of the goats?" Lucas asked.

"Guilty. Do I smell like them?"

It was the first time Lucas had laughed in weeks.

"If you like, I can give you a tour of their little world tomorrow afternoon before vespers. They stink, but they're darlings."

Day four. Tuesday.

Brother Kenneth in the distance looks like a scarecrow. He waves his arm in a grand theatrical arc when he sees me. We have arranged to meet so he can show me the goats, his charges.

Close up, at the end of the hot workday, he is drenched, his thin blue shirt clinging to his bony shoulder blades, and a strong smell of sweat surrounds him like a bee swarm.

In the enclosure, he shows off the goats' obedience when he calls them. "Tammy, Patsy, Roy," he sings out, and the goats come in the order called. "You see I name them after country and western singers because they all sound the same." He lets go of a hooting laugh that I can't help join, infectious as a yawn.

He rubs his bald head periodically, a caress, his armpit an explosion of reek when he raises his arm. I can see he was handsome once, eyes blue like sapphires, a wide, curving mouth that smiles and laughs at everything and reveals even, perfect teeth. He is made of joy.

He has a sister, I know from the other monks. I invent the history I don't know. He gambols on the floor with his nieces and nephews, tickles, makes faces. At the dinner table all eyes are on him. He is a welcome hilarity into their lives of routines, weeks like strung stones, and he the intervening gem.

"Are you single?" he asks.

"No." I don't elaborate. Angie doesn't belong here.

"Lucky person, whoever it is."

He could have said — should have said? —
"woman" or "wife." I am unaccountably delighted by
how he puts it.

The sun is low, and in the amber light his face
grows young. I want to stay at his side late into the
night.

We walk back to the cluster of buildings, the
dorm, the chapel, the mess hall, side by side, si-
lent. Our bare arms brush, the vellus blending and
rousing. He glances my way occasionally with a
knowing smile. In another setting, it would come
across as seductive, and maybe it is, because before
we part ways in the dorm he hugs me. Except that it
is more like an immobilizing clasp, and he gives me
a kiss on the cheek which he holds and holds, as if he
is drinking from my skin, and before I know it he
is gone. His affectionate assault surprises me, as does
my own acquiescence, and more — my need. I have
never been happier.

By the fifth evening, Lucas was growing alarmed about Brother
William's change in attitude. The days were passing fast, and
he was impatient to find a path towards being able to do his
job and continue in his marriage. He pressed Brother William
about the role of punishment in society while they were still
in the dining hall, right after dinner, still surrounded by the
hum of the monks' animated conversations. "Not now," the
monk said.

Afterwards, Lucas went upstairs to the library alone, and
tried to read without success. He was feeling chastised for his

outburst with Brother William, and could not concentrate. Eventually he heard the monk's steps on the stairs, and he stood up, relieved, almost elated.

The monk sat and waved to Lucas' chair. Without preamble, he said, "Punishment is a necessary part of any civilized society. It can set a corrected trajectory for some people."

Lucas squirmed on the hard wooden chair. "But when it's used in place of necessary treatment?"

"No, it doesn't take the place of proper therapy. But it shouldn't be withheld, either, when appropriate."

Brother William then assured him he would direct some of his reading towards the beneficial role of punishment before his week came to a close, and he brought the session to an abrupt end by standing up and saying good night.

As he did most nights after their session, Lucas went to bed and thought about the discussion after he turned the lights out. He was sorry that his mention of 9/11 had triggered a change in Brother William's friendly, accessible manner, and wished now he hadn't brought it up. His regret unsettled him and kept him awake, and he turned the light on again to read.

He opened the biography of Hannah Arendt he had brought with him, the one he hadn't finished reading at home, distracted by the tension with Angie.

He had bookmarked the passages in which her writings were discussed. She believed that political power was possible only by consensus of the population. Hitler, Stalin, Castro were successful totalitarian dictators able to stay in power because of the support of the population they ruled, despite the damaging, sometimes deadly outcomes for many citizens. Punishable evil, by leaders as well as the people, was the result of those thoughtless actions.

He closed the book, and thought about his own life, the desires he had always battled, which were not those of the ruling majority, and which were viewed as deviant. For those desires, he had been punished by a merciless Coach Gomez and made to feel like an outcast by his own father. If he could help it, he did not want to be part of that victimized minority, like a Jew in Germany or a dissident in Russia. He would not lead the sort of life that could result in his spiritual damage or death at the hands of a thoughtless, ruthless population. Heedless annihilation of people who were different was the very definition of punishable evil, if Hannah Arendt was correct, and he was not going to be a casualty of the majority's brutality. He wanted to thrive.

Chapter 15

Product

On Thursday, the sixth day of his retreat, Lucas realized that Brother Kenneth had not been in chapel since their meeting Tuesday evening, and he had not heard his characteristic laugh during meals. After Brother William's change in attitude, Lucas felt isolated despite being surrounded by the other brothers. He wanted to spend more time with Kenneth, a source of comfort and affection.

When Lucas saw Brother James on his way to the potato field in the afternoon, he asked about Kenneth. He knew that James and Kenneth often sat together during meals.

"He's in the hospital again."

"Again? What's wrong?"

"Pneumonia," Brother James said. The monk's eyebrows twitched up. "It's his fourth episode this year. They're doing some extra tests this time, changing some of his medications."

"When you see him, wish him my best, please. I miss seeing him." He refrained from probing, asking about the medications, but he felt an urgency about seeing the monk now that the man was in the hospital. " I hope to see him again before I leave."

Brother James nodded. "Yes, he said he really enjoyed the time you spent together." A big grin, although there was sadness in the man's eyes.

Lucas smiled at the memory of Brother Kenneth's embrace, and the happiness he had felt in the arms of the monk gave him license him to blurt out, "Brother William seems so pre-occupied lately." He was immediately sorry he had mentioned it, hadn't meant to criticize his mentor. He didn't know how this community would view negative comments from a guest.

Brother James nodded and walked away towards the of-fice, which Brother William was exiting. Lucas watched from a distance as the two men exchanged more than just a couple of words while William glanced at Lucas repeatedly. The monks embraced before parting ways.

After dinner that day, their sixth evening of discussion, Brother William suggested they hold their meeting outside instead of in the library. They ambled in the pear orchard as the light began to dim, and the grass under their feet appeared to turn from green to grey on its way to the blackness that night would bring. Bats were swooping and darting overhead. "Good," Brother William said, looking up. "They'll make dinner out of the mosquitoes."

Lucas was relieved that Brother William's casual tone of voice and demeanor had returned. He hoped the strain be-tween them was over for good. The evening air was cooling, although the breeze that blew through the pear trees still felt warm, and carried with it the scent of the ripening fruit. They strolled in silence a few minutes.

"I hear you made a connection with Brother Kenneth." His tone was gentler than Lucas remembered ever hearing.

"I had a nice evening with him. He's a funny man. Loves his goats." He chuckled, then frowned when he remembered Angie's dismissal of the animals.

The monk nodded. "He's a passionate person. Caring." He put his arm around Lucas' shoulders, "Let's talk about home and Angie."

"Something's changed over the years," Lucas said, surprised and comforted by the monk's gesture, as if he was being hugged. Lucas went on to describe their happy early days, and the gradual souring of their home life as he grew dissatisfied with his job. As he spoke, he saw William nod and felt reassured by the weight of his arm. He could trust this man with anything, any revelation about himself or his life. And so the old attractions he had felt for men flitted in his brain, and he considered speaking of them, but he pushed them aside. He still remembered the joy that sex with Angie had brought him years ago. The pleasure of those unions could not be denied, or erased. And yet, the idea that his job was responsible for his marital problems appeared to be receding, replaced by the growing realization of his true sexuality. Still, his trepidation about being ostracized prevented him from accepting the deep and forceful undercurrent of his being. He trusted William, but he did not think the monk would approve of repressing one's true nature to avoid being victimized by society.

"This is why I'm here. If I can justify punishing drug dealers and users, if I can find peace with that, I think I can salvage my relationship with Angie." He spoke softly, sounding unconvincing even to himself.

Brother William shook his head, then said, "Tell me specifically what's making her so unhappy."

Lucas slowed his pace, and looked at Brother William. The monk's eyes were encouraging, as if he already knew that

Lucas was holding on to an important piece of information. Lucas wanted to prolong this moment, hold it suspended, so that he could summon it again in the future if he ever allowed himself to accept the truth of who he was and live by it. "I have lost my sexual interest in her," he said, and they stopped walking and stood looking at each other. "Completely. She thought I was having an affair, because it's been so long since I have wanted sex with her."

"Have you had an affair?"

"No, of course not. I have no interest in other women."

Brother William nodded and looked off into the gloaming for a few seconds.

"Do you have any fantasies then, any form of sexual release?"

Lucas felt flushed then, and his cheeks colored. He was glad the light was dim. The breeze had cooled further, and the scent of pear was gone, replaced by the smell of rich, humid earth. The loamy aroma, perhaps because of this moment of intimacy with Brother William, was soothing, and he took a deep breath. He wanted to suspend the passage of time. "Yes. Sometimes." He knew his voice, just above a whisper, had betrayed him.

Brother William said nothing now, but looked at him a few seconds. "We've sorted out the role of punishment in society. But why would being comfortable with punishing drug traffickers bring back your sexual interest in your wife?"

Lucas had no answer. This was, ostensibly, the reason he had come to the monastery. "I just don't know."

"You said you are sensitive to her needs, and try to accommodate her?"

"Absolutely. I spend a lot of energy doing that at home."

Brother William looked up at the sky and held his gaze there, as if he was looking for bats. But there were none now.

The first stars were beginning to appear. Sirius, the brightest in the northern skies, looked like an approaching, otherworldly vessel.

The monk spoke in the most soothing and gentle voice Lucas had ever heard. "How sensitive are you being to you own needs? The sexual ones I mean. Would Arendt and Augustine approve of your compassion and understanding of your own person?"

He did not wait for an answer, but patted Lucas on the shoulder. "Let's go back." The monk walked towards the chapel for evening prayers.

Lucas was embarrassed by the exchange, and by the inquiry into his sexual fantasies. The air was cool and dry now, but he wiped perspiration from his upper lip. He stood alone in the orchard for several minutes. The crescent moon was rising above the treetops, and looked huge. He knew it was a distortion, a matter of perception and perspective. He had come to find peace at work and at home and stay safe inside society, and Brother William was pushing him in a totally different direction, one that he specifically had not wanted to explore with a therapist.

As he worked the fields the next day, his last full day of the retreat, Lucas tried to sort out all he had discussed with Brother William as he picked the potato beetles off the plants. Instead of putting them in the container with alcohol, as he had been instructed, he held a handful of them and lay them on the soil. He stepped on them, heard and felt a crunch under his shoe, but when he lifted his foot most of the bugs were still alive. Their metallic sheen reminded him of the shiny capsule around a pupa, a dormant caterpillar before it emerges as a butterfly. He knelt to scoop up the beetles to put them in the alcohol. Instead of dropping them into the jar to their deaths, he flung them into the air and wiped his eyes, which had welled up and were wetting his lids. He was not ready to redefine himself, although he could see what the monk was recommending as clearly as he could see the iridescence of the potato beetles as they flew away.

At the toll of the bell, at the end of the afternoon's toil, he walked back to the dormitory. It was the hottest day yet of his stay, and he was parched and starved. He passed the orchard of Moreçau pear trees, and considered plucking one of the low hanging fruit to quench his thirst. The pears were ripe for harvesting, unblemished, and he noticed how much this pinkish variety resembled naked human bodies as Rubens might paint them, with wide, blushing bottoms. He fondled and sniffed one of the dangling fruit. Their weight reminded him of when he touched his own testicles in the privacy of the shower, when he would remember being in the showers and in the locker room with his teammates. He smelled the fruit again. The aroma was reminiscent of something familiar that he could not remember. His hunger made him consider again plucking one off the branch, but he moved on instead to the dormitory to don his gray robe for afternoon prayers.

On his way to chapel a few minutes later, he ran into Brother James, who appeared somber and self-absorbed. There were dark circles under his eyes, and his laugh lines were pulled down, approximating a pout.

"Brother James. Something wrong?"

The monk stopped, glanced at him, and averted his eyes. "Kenneth has passed." His voice was a dry croak. "I'm on my way to the hospital to retrieve the body for burial here."

The orchard and buildings spun. Lucas' legs buckled. He fell to his knees first, then sat on the ground. A wave of nausea forced him to lie down completely, ignoring the wet earth that was muddying his hair and cassock.

"Oh my God." James knelt next to him, picked his head up off the dirt and looked around for help, but Lucas hoisted himself up to sitting, embarrassed.

"I'm okay. Please." He struggled to his knees and stood up.

Brother James put his arm around his waist while Lucas shook some mud off his cassock. The buildings looked askew still, tilting this way and that. He no longer needed the monk's arm for support, but he liked the feel of the gesture.

"I'm so sorry." His vision still blurred, his tongue dry, he felt a vise around his chest. He took a deep breath. "I didn't even know he was ill," he whispered.

Brother James nodded. He hesitated, then said, "He died of pneumonia," without looking at Lucas. "But he also had leukemia. It was all too much."

"So sudden." Lucas took some deep breaths, and his vision began to clear, which was unwelcomed, because he did not want to see anything of the world around him now. He closed his eyes and shook his head, trying to scatter the news from his brain. "Is there anything I can do?"

"Not now, thank you," Brother James said. "But perhaps you can attend the burial in two days."

Lucas thought a moment. Time had flown. "I'm sorry, I'll be gone by then. I'm leaving tomorrow."

The monk nodded. "Of course. I had forgotten. So it will just be our community at the burial." James didn't make a move to go on to prayers, as if he wasn't ready to leave Lucas. His head was turned down, eyes on the pebbled path that led to the chapel.

"Didn't he have a sister?"

Brother James shook his head once, then said, "Well, yes. But she wanted nothing to do with him. We called her with the news, and she doesn't want to come to the burial. It'll be just us."

Lucas frowned, surprised that anyone would shun Brother Kenneth, a cheerful man who had exuded joviality and affection. "Why wouldn't she want to be here to bury him?"

Brother James sighed. "Brother Kenneth had AIDS. No one talked about it, although he didn't want to hide it, particularly. The leukemia was an adverse effect from the medications he took long ago. His sister screamed at him the last time she came to see him, right here, when he told her. She said AIDS was God's punishment for his being gay. Some of us heard her yelling it."

Lucas brought his palms up to his temples and held his head. He spoke to the ground. "How could she? How could anyone be that cruel?" He closed his eyes and felt his throat flooding with rage, and could not suppress a sob at the thought of Kenneth being rejected by family.

James put his arm around him and brought him in for a hug, and while in the monk's arms Lucas wiped his wet cheeks on the man's shoulder.

"It's just as well she's not coming, really," Brother James said. Lucas stepped back from the embrace, wanting to look at the monk's face with this unexpected pronouncement. "We talked about it among us. Brother William didn't even want me to call her with the news, because he didn't want her here."

"I think Brother William was right. If she has that attitude, she shouldn't be given the privilege of burying her brother," Lucas said.

"That's exactly how William put it. He says he's seen this before, the phenomenon of blaming the victim. He studied it as a psychologist, but he's also seen it in his family, and cannot stand the thought of it."

Before dinner, Lucas walked around the grounds instead of retiring to his room. The pear trees were gorgeous with their bounty, although much of the fruit was on the ground already, some of it decaying, preparing to release its seed. A few of the still-attached leaves on the trees were beginning to yellow, auguring the beginning of dormancy.

The memory of Kenneth's persona, the warmth he had received from the monk, displaced everything else, permeated every perception. The death of a man he had known so briefly had left a crater in his chest. If this death felt like such a monumental loss, what would it be like to lose Angie, or his parents? As he considered this, he visualized himself not seeing any of them ever again. He loved the three of them with all his being, but he had a strong sense that life without them would be fully possible, with all of its joys and sorrows, even if their loss was painful at first. He was surprised that he felt what seemed to be a new callousness, but this past week, during which he had not thought about any of them very much, was making that clear. What remained bright within him was what he had felt in Kenneth's embrace, a need for a man's closeness being satisfied.

Back in his room, he riffled through his books, especially the works of Augustine, but could find no mention of the moral justification of going against society's norms. He remembered how Hannah Arendt had framed punishable actions and majority rule, but neither she nor any other great thinker had addressed the range of acceptable human behavior in society. He wanted to focus on this concept at tonight's discussion session, which would be his last. His week's retreat was coming to an end too fast. But where could he read about the nexus between societal standards and sexual variation? He wondered whether it would be an imposition on Brother William to ask his advice now about what to read in preparation for this evening, then remembered that Brother William had encouraged him to seek him out at any time if a pressing question arose.

He took the book in which he had found a reference to human diversity, *Essays on Being,* and walked down the hall in his bare feet to Brother William's door. He knocked lightly, then again more firmly, and got no answer. He would leave Brother William a note and the book open to the chapter "Living with Rules," asking him what else he should read for their discussion after dinner. He opened the door slowly, entered the room, and was struck by the heat, generated by the sun dazzling in through the windows.

Day seven. Friday.

Brother William lies naked, uncovered and asleep in his narrow bed, arms over his head, legs akimbo. The sheers over the open windows hang still, unmoved by any breeze.

I stand by the door a minute and watch the monk breathe, put the book on the dresser and pad to the bed, the man's sinewy body pulling me in, a fish on a line. His underwear is on the floor, next to the bed. I stand on it, my toes curling in the soft cotton, and bend over, my face inches from his chest, watching it rise and fall. My toes curl and grip the briefs when my nose captures a strong blend of sweat and musk. There is furnace heat radiating from the body that I can feel even in the sweltering room. My upper lip is wet with perspiration, and I'm short of breath, maybe because of the intense heat. But there is also an engorgement and a throb deep in my pelvis that I haven't felt in many months. I take off my tee-shirt and drop it, cross my arms, and tuck my hands into my armpits. The moist hair there is confirmation of what I am, mysteriously reassuring. William's breathing changes now from the slow rhythm of deep sleep to that of incipient wakefulness, or perhaps already a dim awareness. I wipe the sweat from my face with my hands and catch my own smell, different than his, but connected, somehow. I scoop my shirt up off the floor, and without taking my eyes off his body I back away towards the door and out of the room.

That evening, during their discussion in the library, Brother William gave no sign that he had been aware of Lucas' presence in his room. Lucas had been expecting a reproach, or a return of the monk's emotional distance. But William's manner remained casual and conversant, and Lucas was relieved. Towards the end of the evening, he summarized the week's exploration of Lucas' questions. They had touched upon the will of the majority, compassion for rule-breakers, and respect for fellow citizens, concepts associated with Hannah Arendt and Augustine.

"Punishment is not counter to moral principles, even in the absence of rehabilitation. When thoughtfully applied, it leads to repentance, and hopefully to change, so that the person who is punished becomes a better person. That answers the dilemma you came to our monastery with."

Lucas nodded. He remembered now he had left his book on William's dresser, and had difficulty looking at the monk, who had to know Lucas had been in the room while he slept.

"In terms of your marital problem, that's a different issue altogether." The monk spoke slowly. "I think we both know that your becoming comfortable with meting out punishment will not return your sexual interest in your wife."

The monk paused and looked up at the ceiling above Lucas' head. "We mentioned sexual fantasies last evening, and being understanding not just of others, but of yourself. Have you given that some thought?"

Lucas nodded, but said nothing. He wasn't ready to translate the tendrils of his new self-knowledge into words.

"Reflect on what your own needs are. Make the necessary adjustments, maybe with Angie, maybe not." William looked at him and held his palms open in front of him, as if extending an offering. It was an odd gesture, Lucas thought, and he wondered whether the monk was offering his hands for him to hold in some version of fraternal communion.

Lucas kept his hands clasped on the table and said nothing, looking at the space between them, unable to focus on the face in front of him.

Brother William stood up and smiled. "You know, since you majored in philosophy, you may remember that one of Kierkegaard's tenets was that in order to be true to yourself, you often have to go against the majority." He started towards the stairs. "I'll drive you to the station tomorrow, and we'll say good-bye then."

That evening, his last at the monastery, Lucas walked the grounds after vespers instead of going back to his room. There moon had not yet risen, and the lights from the windows of the dorm and chapel seemed too bright, intruding into his need for contemplation. He walked away from the structures and into the orchards. Gusts of a restless breeze made his grey cassock swing and snap around his ankles, and he stumbled over the unseen, uneven terrain. But he walked on, away from the buildings, unsure where the monastery ended and where the outside world began. He was unaware of how much time had passed when he came upon a fence of aluminum posts and cattle wire. Lucas could hear a rushing a stream or a river, but he couldn't see in the dense darkness. He didn't venture beyond the fence, despite the inviting sound of the water. He wanted to remain within the safe bounds of the monastery, and walked further along the fence until he came to the edge of what he recognized as his potato field. The loamy fragrance was as familiar and comforting as that of baby powder.

He stood amongst the rows of plants, and felt a great but what he thought was absurd pride that his work had resulted in the lush productivity he knew was all around him but could not see. Still, there was an energy he could feel from the plantings, almost like the buzzing of bees. He wondered who would tend to the potatoes tomorrow, after he was gone. Lucas smiled and shook his head when he remembered that the potato plants had been there before his arrival, and would continue on without him. He thought then with some unease that he would be on the train back to New York in the morning instead of here, among his plants. And he remembered that he would be seeing Angie again, about which he felt nothing. No anticipation, no trepidation. He was aware that his love for her was there still, but different now, distant. He felt an uplifting freedom now to love her on his own terms.

He went back to the chapel, and instead of going to his usual pew, near the rear, sat close to the altar and the enormous, looming cross. Incense lingered in the air. The cross was almost as large as he was, carved out of a blond, deeply grained wood, and when he looked at it he saw an austere but elegant object. Lucas considered its strength and immutability. He thought about the conversation in the orchard last night, about his sexual fantasies, and tonight's discussion as well, about being fair to himself. "It is what it is," he said out loud, looking at the massive cross that held no religious meaning for him, and yet existed on its own terms, unaffected by anyone's opinion of it. It simply was.

Back in his room, he began to pack, and found under-wear that didn't belong to him rolled up inside the tee shirt he had worn earlier. He must have picked up Brother William's briefs along with his own shirt off the floor in the monk's room. He didn't see how he could return the garment without an impossibly awkward explanation, and considered leaving it in the closet of his room, but he folded it and packed it along with his own clothes. He wondered whether William had been aware of his presence. Had he remained purposefully exposed? Lucas could have made his presence known. But then what?

He went to bed, and fell asleep instantly and deeply.

At eight the next morning he went to the administrative office, where he expected to meet Brother William for the ride to the train station. Instead, he found Brother James waiting for him. "Brother William had some business this morning and couldn't drive you. Off we go," the burly monk said, then helped Lucas with his duffel bags into the blue pickup.

"Brother William sends his farewell and good wishes." James glanced at Lucas as he put the truck in gear.

They rode mostly in silence, looking out over the green valleys and gray mountains illuminated by a bright, diffuse sunlight behind thin clouds. As they made the final descent into the cornfields, Lucas said, "I was hoping to see Brother William today. I really needed to say something to him."

"Do you want me to give him a message?"

Lucas thought a moment. "Please tell him I apologize."

Brother James looked mildly puzzled. "Will he know for what?"

"I'm not sure. Maybe. I trespassed on his privacy."

The monk nodded. "As a matter of fact, Brother William has a message for you, too, as well as an apology."

Lucas turned in his seat to look at the monk. "What is it?" His upper lip began to perspire.

"He apologizes for his gruffness with you when you mentioned 9/11." Brother James made the final turn on to the road leading to the train station. "And he also gave me permission to divulge something about his past, something that many even in our community don't know about."

Lucas held his breath. He was imagining something about Brother William that would echo his own needs and fantasies, a mirroring of his sexuality from someone he admired.

"He lost his fiancée in the twin towers during the 9/11 attacks. He said you struck a sensitive spot when you spoke of it, and he's sorry he reacted so unkindly."

Lucas faced front in his seat again as they approached the station.

"No." Lucas shook his head. "That's not what I was expecting."

"Yes," Brother James said, "it's not widely known in our community."

Lucas ignored the non-intersecting exchange. "I wonder now if he would have known what I was going to apologize about."

Brother James chuckled as he pulled the pickup into the train station, scattering some geese. "Brother William is a very compassionate man, and insightful as well. He made reference to your trespass, as you call it, and didn't seem upset by it. He found the book you left on his dresser." The monk turned the engine off and shifted in his seat to look at Lucas, gazing at him in the same penetrating way Brother William had often done, the look he now understood signaled caring. James nodded and patted him on the knee as he got out of the truck.

"Your train will be here soon." Brother James set Lucas' bags down on the wooden platform. "I have to get back for Brother Kenneth's burial." There was no one else at the station. He gave Lucas a hug, then said, "Brother William said to tell you that he was really sorry he couldn't say a proper good-bye to you. He thought this way would be best, and he said you should be patient, that the week you have spent with us will help you." He turned and started walking back to the truck, but halfway there he stopped and turned around. "He spoke highly of you all these days, you know, said you're a man of conscience. I guess you struck a chord with him." He said this louder than he needed to, close to a shout, and dozens of crows in the cornfield took off, a rush of black flurry that gave way to a cloud-speckled sky. Brother James got into the truck and honked a good-bye as he drove away.

The kindness stayed with him throughout the train ride home, a mist of calm. He opened his bag looking for his book, and saw the monk's underwear. As he picked it up to re-fold it and place it among his own, he caught the familiar scent of musky sweat. It filled him with a strange serenity, and an unmistakable sense of transition.

He resolved to minimize the pain he would have to in-flict, because he loved her, and did not want her hate, or to be completely estranged from her. She had already been punished enough for falling in love with him, and then wanting to marry him.

He arrived at their apartment building, and came to the familiar green door in the hallway. He inched it open and stepped inside. The apartment appeared more spacious and brighter than he remembered. She came into view through the kitchen door with a glass of wine in her hand, smiling, wearing shorts and a pink tank top. He felt great relief that he no longer had to respond. Lucas set his duffel bags down and embraced her like a man saying good-bye to his sister. The fragrance of her pear shampoo would remain unforgettable.

Acknowledgements

Chapter 1, "The Underwear Hat," appeared as a short story in the *Atticus Review* anthology. Parts of chapters 14, "Retreat," and 15 "Product," appeared as a short story titled "Retreat" in *Turk's Head Review*.

About the Author

José Sotolongo is a physician, born in Cuba. He practiced medicine until 2011, then devoted himself to fiction and poetry full time, although he's been writing since childhood. He got his first rejection from the *Reader's Digest* at age eleven for his initial effort in English, an account of the day he left his country by flying from Havana to Miami, age ten, without his parents. His fiction and poetry have appeared in several publications, including Bloody Key Society, Opossum, Leafland, and New Reader Magazine, as well as in The Peacock Journal, Atticus Review, and Love Like Salt anthologies. He and his spouse make their home on an old goat farm in the Catskills of New York. In between battling the woodchucks and rabbits that ransack his vegetable garden, he works on completing a short story collection.

www.ingramcontent.com/pod-product-compliance
Lightning Source LLC
Chambersburg PA
CBHW030832020726
47499CB00006B/2162